SUMMER HAWK

Down from the Black Hills he came.

Out of the caves where crystal spires gave off the
    light
    of a million stars.

Into the mountains he flew, soaring on mighty wings.

Hawk.

Mysterious and powerful,

Healer,

Lover,

Father,

Friend.

With wings outspread he covered his love, and up from
    her womb sprang his children:

Strong sons and a daughter with eyes
    the color of the sky.

Dear Reader,

It's going to be a wonderful year! After all, we're celebrating Silhouette's 20th anniversary of bringing you compelling, emotional, contemporary romances month after month.

January's fabulous lineup starts with beloved author Diana Palmer, who returns to Special Edition with *Matt Caldwell: Texas Tycoon*. In the latest installment of her wildly popular LONG, TALL TEXANS series, temperatures rise and the stakes are high when a rugged tycoon meets his match in an innocent beauty—who is also his feisty employee.

Bestselling author Susan Mallery continues the next round of the series PRESCRIPTION: MARRIAGE with *Their Little Princess*. In this heart-tugging story, baby doctor Kelly Hall gives a suddenly single dad lessons in parenting—and learns all about romance!

Reader favorite Pamela Toth launches Special Edition's newest series, SO MANY BABIES—in which babies and romance abound in the Buttonwood Baby Clinic. In *The Baby Legacy*, a sperm-bank mix-up brings two unlikely parents together temporarily—or perhaps forever....

In Peggy Webb's passionate story, *Summer Hawk*, two Native Americans put aside their differences when they unite to battle a medical crisis and find that love cures all. Rounding off the month is veteran author Pat Warren's poignant, must-read secret baby story, *Daddy by Surprise*, and Jean Brashear's *Lonesome No More*, in which a reclusive hero finds healing for his heart when he offers a single mom and her young son a haven from harm.

I hope you enjoy these six unforgettable romances and help us celebrate Silhouette's 20th anniversary all year long!

Best,

Karen Taylor Richman
Senior Editor

Please address questions and book requests to:
Silhouette Reader Service
U.S.: 3010 Walden Have., P.O. Box 1325, Buffalo, NY 14269
Canadian: P.O. Box 609, Fort Erie, Ont. L2A 5X3

PEGGY WEBB
SUMMER HAWK

Silhouette®

SPECIAL ▼ EDITION®

Published by Silhouette Books
America's Publisher of Contemporary Romance

This one's for you, Mama.

Acknowledgments: Dr. Kirsten Patterson, for information on Arbo viruses.

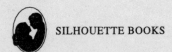 SILHOUETTE BOOKS

ISBN 0-373-24300-6

SUMMER HAWK

Copyright © 2000 by Peggy Webb

Visit us at www.romance.net

Printed in U.S.A.

PEGGY WEBB

and her two chocolate labs live in a hundred-year-old house not far from the farm where she grew up. "A farm is a wonderful place for dreaming," she says. "I used to sit in the hayloft and dream of being a writer." Now, with two grown children and more than forty-five romance novels to her credit, the former English teacher confesses she's still a hopeless romantic and loves to create the happy endings her readers love so well.

When she isn't writing, she can be found at her piano playing blues and jazz or in one of her gardens planting flowers. A believer in the idea that a person should never stand still, Peggy recently taught herself carpentry.

IT'S OUR 20th ANNIVERSARY!
We'll be celebrating all year,
starting with these fabulous titles,
on sale in January 2000.

Chapter One

Callie came upon them unexpectedly, the two people sitting beside a sparkling stream just off a trail deep in the White Mountains. The woman sat with her arms linked around the man's waist, her head resting on his shoulder, and he was looking down at her, his head slightly bent, the lines in his bronzed face softened and his eyes shining with love. Callie had to turn her face away to keep from crying.

Her parents. Age sat like snow on their hair but had left untouched the most vital part of them—their spirits and their hearts.

Drawing her Appaloosa to a halt behind a stand of white birches, Callie sat quietly, not spying but merely unwilling to intrude.

"Remember when I first brought you to this mountain, Ellen?"

In spite of his age, her father's voice was strong and resonant, filled with the musical cadences of the Apache.

"As if it were yesterday, Calder. When I first saw you on your white stallion I thought you were the most magnificent man I'd ever met. I still do."

When she smiled at her husband the years fell away, and Ellen was once more the impish young woman who breached all the defenses of a young Apache doctor caught between two worlds. The force of their passion made the very air around them shimmer. With something almost like reverence, Calder Red Cloud cupped his wife's face.

"And you are still my beautiful Yellow Star."

Callie dug the heels of her soft moccasins into the Appaloosa's side and tangled her hands in his mane, guiding him with silent commands backward out of the trees and away from the bank of the stream. Her parents never even saw her.

The wind caught her tears and threw them back in her face. By the time Callie got to the stables she was a weeping wreck.

She gave her face an angry swipe with the back of her hand, then dismounted and groomed her horse, trying not to think about love so beautiful it made her weep, trying not to think about nights that were so lonely she couldn't even dream, trying not to think about a virus so deadly it killed her best friend.

Introspective by nature, analytical by training, Callie could no more turn off her mind than she could stop breathing. Jennifer was there, deep in the shadows, laughing as they prepared to go into Biolevel Four where the hot viruses were kept, laughing because she was getting too fat for her safety suit.

Callie went inside her parents' sunny kitchen to make

herself a peanut-butter-and-jelly sandwich. Food always helped restore her sense of equilibrium. Jennifer used to tease her about it.

"How come you eat like a horse and I'm the one getting big as a barrel?" she'd say.

Pushing the memory from her mind, Callie wandered into the den to check for telephone messages. The red light was blinking.

"Callie, this is Ron. Call me. I'll be at the center until I hear from you."

A specialist in virulent diseases, she didn't have to wonder what the phone call meant. Her work with hot viruses was dangerous and stressful. Vacation was more than time away from the job: it was emotional and mental recovery. The director for the Center of Disease Control would never call her except in case of emergency.

She picked up the phone and dialed.

"How's it going, kid?" Sixty-five, fatherly and jovial, Dr. Ron Messenger never failed to show his interest in and love for the intrepid team of scientists and doctors under his command.

"Great." Grinning Callie glanced down at her trademark white shirt and jeans, the only clothes she considered necessary for her life-style. "I've gone native since I got home. I'm dressed in war paint and feathers."

"Damn, I wish I wasn't so old." His laughter echoed over the line, then he sobered. "Hate to do this, kid, but pack your bag. You're going to Houston."

"Research?"

"Containment…if God smiles on us."

"In Houston, Texas?" The consequences of failure were mind-boggling. "My god. What happened?"

"A Sudanese, working one of the oil tankers that came into port." Adrenaline pumped through Callie's body as

Ron briefly outlined the situation. "There's no time to lose, Callie."

"I understand."

"Peg Cummings will be prepared to leave the minute you get to Atlanta. You'll be joined in Houston by Dr. Joseph Swift of the National Institute of Virology."

"I'd rather work with the devil himself. Can we request somebody else?"

"It's not like you to listen to gossip, Callie."

Callie knew all the stories, some of them true, some of them pure fabrication—tales of Joseph Swift's legendary temper, his icy demeanor, his lone-wolf ways, his ancestry. But it wasn't the stories that bothered her—it was the man himself. Dr. Joseph Swift was actually Joseph Swift Hawk, a man who denied his Sioux heritage, a man who never used his Sioux name. For that Callie could not forgive him.

"This is personal, Ron."

"Have you two been lovers?"

"I've never even met the man."

"Good. I won't worry about you, then. Sorry about the trip, kid."

"That's okay, Ron. I'll be on the next plane."

"Good. Peg's husband is worried about this being her first field trip. I told him you'd look after her."

"Peg's good, Ron. She doesn't need looking after."

"I know that. But it made him feel better."

"Husbands."

"Yeah, kid. Be glad you don't have one."

Most times she was. But there were times, such as the moment beside the stream observing her parents, when Callie felt a great aching void that threatened to swallow her.

After she hung up she picked up her sandwich, but she'd lost her taste for peanut butter.

"Callie?"

"In here, Mom."

Ellen came through the door, her face flushed and shining, twigs clinging to her clothes and a leaf tangled in her hair. Callie's heart hurt.

"Where's Dad?"

"Gone to the clinic. Said he didn't trust those two young doctors he'd hired."

Ellen gave her daughter a speculative look, but Callie refused to get into that old argument. When she got her medical degree everyone in the family, including her brother Steve, expected her to come home and go into practice with her father. Not that they would ever try to tell her what to do. Still, from time to time Ellen pressed the daughter she called her wild child to come home and work so Calder could retire with peace of mind.

"He'll be seventy-five next month, you know," Ellen added.

"I know."

"I thought I'd throw a big party for him, put up a tent, hire a band, invite all the Mississippi relatives. You can help me plan it after dinner."

"Mom, I won't be here for dinner. The center called."

Ellen's hands shook as she tucked a stray curl into her French twist.

"You'll be back for Calder's birthday, won't you, Callie?"

Callie knew what waited for her in Houston for she'd been there before…something so far removed from birthdays and garden parties that thinking about it sometimes gave her nightmares.

She didn't know when she would come back, or even

if she would come back. But she wasn't about to say that to her mother.

"I'll try, Mom. I really will."

Everything about Houston was large in scale, from the stadium to the Galleria to the glass-and-concrete high-rises that competed with planes for space in the sky.

Joseph sat in a stiff chair at Gate 22 in the airport trying to block out the noise—the din of endless chatter from the river of travelers flowing down the hallways, the drone of planes, the blaring of the loudspeaker. After years of working in remote parts of the world, mostly Africa, he was much more at home with the sounds from the rain forest, the scuffle and chatter of colobus monkeys, the constant drone of insects, the occasional trumpet of a lone elephant, rare now with the noose of civilization slowly strangling its habitat.

The plane was twenty minutes late, and every minute was crucial. Somewhere in the bowels of Houston lurked a disease so deadly it could wipe out the entire city.

If news of what he was doing in Houston got out, panic would spread like wildfire. Only the mayor and the hospital directors knew. So far he'd been able to keep the news media at bay.

"Yes, a small section of the city is quarantined," he'd told a reporter for last night's interview. "It's merely a precautionary measure."

With the area tightly cordoned and police keeping twenty-four hour watch to see that no one entered and no one exited, how long would it be before somebody started probing? How long before somebody leaked the truth?

The last thing he needed was to be wasting time in an airport.

Suddenly there was a flurry as the plane taxied in and family and friends rushed toward the gate.

Joseph didn't join the rush. Long ago he'd abandoned the habit of haste. Living as he did surrounded by the most deadly viruses in the world, he'd learned the beauty of savoring…moments, music, good food, good wine and sweet women.

Callie Red Cloud was the first to emerge from the plane. She could be no other. Her cheekbones and the golden hue of her skin spoke of her Apache heritage. But it was the danger in her that spoke directly to Joseph Swift. Danger was in the sparkle of her eyes, the fetching disarray of her long black hair, the outward thrust of her chin. Callie the Unattainable, his colleagues called her.

"Watch out for her, Joe," Benjamin Dunn had told him before he left for Houston. "She'll get under your skin quicker than an *arbo* virus. But I dare you to try to do anything about it. The lady always says no."

"You have to ask first, Ben. I don't plan to ask."

Joseph never mixed business with pleasure. A pity. Callie Red Cloud might turn out to be a woman worth breaking the rules for.

He knew there was another member of the team, Peg Cummings, but she was nothing more than a vague shadow, blond and petite, bringing up the rear. He only had eyes for Callie.

She was slender, impossibly long legged, incredibly luscious. There was nothing subtle about her beauty. Her body was gorgeous and ripe, her waist slender, hardly more than a handspan.

She stopped in front of him, placing her suitcase and medical bag at her feet, her hands on her hips. Quietly he finished his perusal. She'd didn't move, didn't blink, but matched him stare for stare.

"Dr. Swift, I presume?"

There was something unnerving about the cold formal manner she delivered her greeting, something totally at odds with the woman herself, with the way she dressed, the way she looked. Joseph knew his reputation as a cold fish was widespread, but he hardly thought it deserved such contempt.

"You must be Callie."

"You may call me Dr. *Red Cloud*." She challenged him with a look. "Those are the rules."

"I live by one set of rules, Callie. My own."

Her chin tilted upward. Blue eyes clashed with black.

"If we are to work together, Dr. Swift—"

"Joseph. And you've just defined our relationship, Dr. Red Cloud. Strictly business."

He bent to pick up her suitcase, but she was too fast for him.

"Stop," she said, capturing him with one look from her startling blue eyes. "I always take care of myself."

That a single glance could wield such power took him by surprise. He'd thought he was immune. In fact, he'd taken all precaution to ensure immunity. And now this incredibly lovely Apache witch had breached years of defenses. Late at night when he was alone in his narrow cot he would ponder how such a thing was possible.

"See that you do, Callie. You're too valuable to lose."

Of course he'd meant "too valuable to lose as a doctor," but under her intense scrutiny, his words took on an entirely different meaning.

The arrival of Dr. Peg Cummings saved them from themselves. That's how Joseph viewed the situation. Callie displayed the same relief that he felt.

"Peg, what took you so long?" Callie said.

"Short legs and an out-of-shape body." She extended

her hand to her colleague. "Hi, you must be Dr. Swift. I'm Peg Cummings."

"A pleasure." He bent over her hand and kissed it.

"Hey…" She giggled. "Wait till I tell my husband I'm stranded in Houston with a charmer."

"Will he be jealous?"

Joseph's curiosity was both intellectual and personal. He never ceased to be amazed at the complexity of something that looked so simple: the male-female relationship. There always seemed to be a treachery or deceit going on. What he'd once had didn't fit the pattern.

"Mike? Jealous? He'll think I'm making the whole thing up just to get a rise out of him. Literally."

Her laughter was infectious, and a perfect antidote for what lay waiting for them.

"I'll show you to the car." He took Peg's arm. "Watch your step, Callie," he called over his shoulder. "These airports can be treacherous."

"Save your concern for somebody else, Dr. *Swift*. I've been known to take scalps. I come from hardy Native American stock."

"Apache, to be exact."

She was startled he knew that much about her, but recovered quickly.

"Curiosity or research?"

He turned around. "Neither. Survival. I even know the kind of toothpaste you use."

Callie nodded, her instant understanding confirmation of what he already knew: she was keenly intelligent, the most brilliant virologist Atlanta had to offer. They both knew the enemy they were facing took no prisoners. Their only weapons against a hot agent were knowledge and the colleagues on their teams.

"I will never let you down," she said.

When she lifted her shining eyes to his, Joseph knew that what lay in their depths was far more dangerous than anything that awaited him in the quarantined area. Unable to resist, he caught her hand. It was small boned and beautifully shaped, but he could feel her strength just beneath the surface of the golden skin.

Turning her hand over he studied the crisscrossing of veins. Up close she smelled like exotic flowers.

"Nor I, you," he said.

For one brief electric moment their eyes locked and held, then he released her and charged toward the car.

Chapter Two

Callie stared after the retreating figure of Dr. Joseph Swift. When she was nine years old she and her brother had sneaked out one evening to ride their horses against their parents' orders. A sudden storm had flooded the river separating them from home, and she and Eric had been trapped overnight. They took refuge in a cave until Calder rescued them the next day.

It had been a terrifying experience, but not nearly as terrifying as the one she'd just gone through. She'd felt the shock of Joseph all the way to her heart.

Who was going to rescue her now? That thought blocked out all else as they drove through Houston to the Hispanic barrio on the east side of the city.

Their headquarters was just ahead, two large trailers, which served as research center and dining hall, with two smaller trailers off to the side for sleeping quarters. Dr.

Swift opened the door of one of the smaller trailers, and Peg vanished inside.

Callie dallied, torn by conflicting thoughts.

"Is anything wrong?" Joseph asked.

"No."

The last thing she wanted was for this man to think she had one iota of personal interest in him, one ounce of feeling other than contempt for the way he denied his heritage. True, he was reputed to be one of the most brilliant virologists working today, but he'd have to earn respect.

"I was just thinking about the battle ahead of us."

She looked at the surrounding area, building after building, so much humanity per square inch that a hot virus running rampant could fell thousands in one day.

"It would be daunting to some, but I suspect that you are a woman who is never daunted."

Her eyes swung back to him, the face that looked as if it had been carved from granite, the wild tangle of black hair, the broad chest, the strong legs.

"No, never." It was only a small lie, and she crossed her fingers behind her back the way she had when she was a child.

"The night comes swiftly, Callie, and the darkness can be dangerous in this part of town."

"So I've heard."

"You don't want to be caught alone in the dark."

It wasn't the prospect of being alone in the dark that had her quaking inside like an aspen. She tightened her grip on both her bag and her common sense.

"I don't intend to, Doctor." She walked toward her trailer, her proud posture daring him to say another word. Turning back, she leveled the playing field with one glance. "I have better things to do than fumble around in the dark."

"Somehow I don't think of you as the fumbling kind."

"That's something you'll never find out." She regretted the words the minute they were out of her mouth. Someday her quick wit was going to be her undoing.

The glints in his eyes were not laughter but something far more dangerous.

"It's my loss."

Until that moment Callie had known only two men who could bewitch with words—her father and her brother. Combining the lyricism of Athabascan with the poetry in their souls, they could persuade the sun to come down from the sky or the ocean to give up its tides. Where the fairer sex was concerned, their tongues were lethal weapons.

Apparently the Apache had nothing over the Sioux.

"I'm vaccinated against all deadly viruses," she said, "measles, diptheria, typhoid, insincerity."

Joseph roared with laughter. "Nothing invigorates me more than an agile-minded, tart-tongued woman."

Glancing across the barriers at the section of the city that had become a battleground against a deadly enemy, he sobered. "If you can keep that lively sense of humor in the days ahead, it could be the salvation of us all."

She stared in the direction he was looking, but the sun suddenly dropped as if it had been shot from the sky, and a curtain of darkness descended over the city.

Joseph offered his arm, and this time Callie took it.

"Don't let go," he said.

Was the double entendre deliberate, or was fatigue playing tricks on Callie's mind? "Just tired," she told herself. Tomorrow she would view Joseph strictly as a colleague.

Peg had turned on all the lights inside their trailer, and together Callie and Joseph walked toward the glow. She could barely see his face, but she had no trouble at all feeling his body heat. It came from him in waves, searing her mouth, parching her throat, melting her flesh and bones until she was nothing but a puddle of emotion.

When they reached the door, they paused just outside the pool of lamplight. He stood too close. She held on too long. Neither of them could move.

"Callie…"

She shut her eyes, letting the music of his voice wash over her. She sensed rather than saw his small movement, felt the touch of his fingertips against her cheek, softly, ever so briefly, like the kiss of a butterfly wing.

"Get a good night's sleep," he said. "Tomorrow will be a long day."

And then he was gone, swallowed up by the blackness. His touch lingered on her skin, and she kept her eyes closed for a while, breathing deeply and evenly.

"Callie?" Peg called. "Is that you?"

"It's me."

Peg emerged from the bathroom, her hair tousled and her eyes droopy with fatigue.

"What are you doing standing out here?"

"Would you believe admiring the view?"

"No."

"I thought not." Callie went inside and tossed her bag beside Peg's. "How're you holding up, pal?"

"Better than you. Just look at you."

"What?"

"All swoony and misty-eyed."

"Jet lag."

"He lit your fire. Not that I blame you one little bit. If it weren't for this…" Peg held up the hand with her wedding band. "I'd be consumed by the flames of passion myself."

"There's no such things as flames of passion."

"What about your parents? You're always talking about how much they love each other?"

"That's different. They don't make love like that anymore." Callie unzipped her bag and pulled out the oversize white cotton gown she used for sleeping. "You want me to turn out the light?"

"Sure."

Callie reached toward the switch. "What are you grinning about?"

"Nothing. I'm just grinning, that's all." Peg climbed into her bunk. "Sweet dreams, Callie. And may they all be about sex."

"You are evil and must be destroyed," Callie said. She doused the light, then lay in her bed listening to the sounds of the restless city—a swish of tires on pavement, the blaring of horns, the yelling of impatient cab drivers. And from somewhere nearby, the plaintive music of a guitar.

She turned on her side, pulled aside the curtain and stared out the small window. In the soft glow of lamplight, Joseph was silhouetted against the stark white walls of his trailer, dark head bent forward, guitar cradled in his arms like a lover, fingers moving rapidly along the neck as he shaped his minor chords.

The song ended and he laid down his guitar, then stood up and stretched, magnificently naked, wonderfully formed.

"What demons haunt you?" she whispered.

As if he'd heard, as if he could see her lying in her bed wondering, Joseph turned and stared in the direction of

her trailer. Even across the distance she could feel the heat
of his gaze.

Callie shivered. Then lying back, she closed her eyes.
For once in her life she was going to squelch her natural
curiosity. It didn't matter what demons haunted Dr. Joseph Swift. Dr. Callie Red Cloud was planning to put her
mind to other things.

Joseph was making coffee when Callie emerged from
her trailer the next morning. Yesterday had not been a
dream. In the unforgiving light of day, even without
makeup and still suffering from jet lag, she was quite
simply the most sensational-looking woman he'd ever
seen. But it was more than her looks that electrified him.
It was the sensation of walking through his old neighborhood and discovering that the villa where he'd laughed
and loved had suddenly been resurrected from the ashes.

"Good morning," she called, striding toward him, rolling up the cuffs of her white shirt.

When she entered the temporary mess hall his mind
jolted back to the chore at hand, and he finished measuring coffee grounds into the pot, then turned his attention
to the skillet.

"Breakfast is almost ready."

"I didn't expect you to cook."

He lifted the charred bacon with a spatula. "I hate it,
but here we do what's necessary. The fewer people we
involve in this matter, the better. Today is my shift, tomorrow is yours."

"If there is a tomorrow," she said. "How bad is it over
there?" She nodded in the direction of the barricades.

"Still contained. I'll brief you as soon as Peg arrives."

"Am I late?" Peg rushed through the door, still buttoning her blouse. "I wanted to make a good impression on my first field trip."

"Impressions don't count here," Joseph said.

In the purple dawn, he finished cooking, then briefed them over breakfast. He told how Simba Kunte had brought the virus to his cousin's house in the barrio, how he had refused to go to a doctor, how quickly the hot virus spread.

"By the time it had been identified, fifteen in the barrio were stricken. That number is now thirty-seven, but holding. We've had no new cases in the last two days."

"What about the tanker?" Callie asked.

"It's still under quarantine. Only two developed mild cases, and they are on the road to recovery. As you know, transfer of this virus occurs in the acute stage. Putting a city the size of Houston under quarantine would not only be counterproductive, it would create widespread panic and probably rioting or worse. We can only pray that the stricken ones have been too sick to travel outside their own homes and neighborhoods."

Both women asked intelligent, pertinent questions. But the true test would come when they crossed the barriers and went into the field hospital.

"Any other questions?" he asked, and they responded, no. "Then let's suit up."

Joseph never entered a quarantined area without thinking about his wife, Maria, of the laughing dark eyes and the skin as hot as volcanic ash. How happy they had once been, how arrogant in their presumption that their knowledge and skill could protect them, how totally unprepared for tragedy.

She'd died on the Ivory Coast. Joseph and Maria, the unbeatable team had been beaten by the virus they'd gone in to fight. One small mistake, a mask that had slipped out of place. One small opening, an entrance for a virus so deadly it needed nothing more than a pinpoint to invade and destroy its host.

He'd fought until the bitter end, and at the last all he could do was hold her hand and silently curse the fates for taking her...and himself for letting her die. He should have never let her come into the midst of an outbreak. He should never have let her go down into the village. He should have been more careful, more vigilant.

His list of sins and shortcomings went on and on, but nothing could bring her back. And nothing could bring him to mix business with pleasure. Ever again.

Then why did his heart contract when he saw Callie Red Cloud striding toward him in her safety suit? Why did he want to rush forward and carry her away from this place of damnation?

"Ready for inspection, Doctor," she said, her voice crisp and full of confidence.

Joseph hardened his heart. Callie was a professional, just as he was. She was a member of the team. Nothing more.

Peg joined her, and he inspected every detail of their suits, from the tape wrapping their wrists and ankles to seal the gaskets, to their boots and gloves, to the fit of their face masks and the seals of the helmets.

On the first inspection he found nothing amiss, but he did it again just to be certain. Hidden in the voluminous pressurized safety suit, nothing but her face visible, Callie still had the power to render him breathless.

Silently damning himself for letting his emotions threaten his good sense, he gave the all-clear signal, and the three of them passed the quarantine lines into the stricken barrio of Houston.

Chapter Three

No matter how often she saw the effects of one of the hot viruses, Callie never failed to be moved at the sight. The temporary hospital was a huge warehouse, well equipped and staffed by two local doctors and three nurses, nuns who had flown in from a hospital in San Antonio to fight the outbreak. Saints, all.

And around them lay the sick, helpless and hopeless.

Callie blinked back tears, and then she checked on Peg. Her face was ashen and her knees threatened to buckle. Callie put her hand on her friend's arm.

"Are you okay?"

"My God. I never dreamed it would be so horrible."

Callie led her outside.

"Take deep breaths."

"That child! Did you see that little boy?"

"I saw him."

Peg bent double. "I don't know if I can do this."

"The first time is always the hardest."

"Does it get better?"

"No, it never gets better. You just get stronger, that's all."

"What's going on out here?" Ice was warmer than Joseph's voice.

Callie whirled around. "It's her first time."

"Then let her deal with it. I don't have time for you to play nursemaid to a perfectly healthy woman when we have a hospital full of the dying."

"Don't you have a heart?"

"I can't afford a heart." He turned back toward the hospital, calling over his shoulder. "Are you coming, Dr. Red Cloud?"

She gave him a smart salute, then with one last reassuring squeeze to Peg's arm, she marched inside.

"I'll wire for a replacement for her tomorrow." Joseph handed Callie a handful of charts. "And don't give me that look. In this business, nobody gets a second chance."

"You didn't even give her a first chance." Callie was so furious she had a hard time controlling the quaver in her voice.

"It's all right, Callie." Peg appeared in the doorway. "I can speak for myself." She faced Joseph. "It won't happen again, Dr. Swift."

He studied her for a long moment, then handed charts to her.

"Let's get to work, then."

To all appearances Joseph was completely focused on his work: only he knew of his inner turmoil. Callie was bending over the bed of the small boy who had stolen Joseph's heart days earlier. Ricardo Valesquez, four years old and fighting like a tiger cub against the insidious virus that racked his small body, lay in the bed closest to the doorway, for even in his feeble state he insisted on seeing the light.

What was he thinking, lying there watching the shadow-play as the sun tracked across the sky? Was he thinking that only a week ago he'd been running through his neighborhood playing ball with his friends? Was he remembering how he tried to sink a goal in the net that was far too tall for him? Was he remembering his parents, struck down in their prime by the *arbo* virus that sneaked into the barrio like a thief, stealing the brightest and the best?

Everything about Callie conveyed her tenderness and compassion—touch, tone, body language.

"Don't you worry, little one. We're going to take good care of you." She stroked him with her gloved hand, brushing the dark hair from eyes suddenly grown too big for the fever-flushed face.

"But you have to help us. You have to fight. Do you understand? Fight, little one. Fight."

Suddenly Joseph was spinning through time and space, hearing another voice, seeing another woman, another child. The language was different but the words were the same.

"Fight, my darling, fight," Maria had said in Italian, and then she'd bent down and placed a kiss on the stricken child's forehead.

A fatal kiss. The child, already too far gone had died in the night, and Maria, his love, his life, had allowed passage of the deadly virus into her safety suit when she bent to kiss the child.

Joseph had seen what was happening, saw the face

mask slip ever so slightly, saw the fatal opening between mask and hood.

"Maria!" He'd raced across the room, jerking her mask back into place, but it was already too late.

Helpless, he'd watched the virus consume his wife. Neither his medicine nor his prayers could keep her alive. And neither his tears nor his curses could bring her back.

He'd laid her to rest in the green hills of Umbria she'd loved so deeply. Then he'd locked up his heart.

Young and arrogant when they'd married, as full of life as they were of love, they'd thought it could never happen to them. And yet it had.

Joseph shook his head to clear away the memories. Callie finished recording the small boy's temperature, then she brushed back Ricardo's hair and bent over his bed.

"Callie!" Joseph felt as if he were running in slow motion, too late to help her, too late to prevent another disaster.

Callie jerked around, eyes as bright as blue flames through the mask. He gripped her upper arm, his eyes scanning her mask for signs of slippage.

"What are you doing?" he said.

"Straightening his pillow." She looked at his hand, still held in a death grip on her arm. "What are you doing?"

"Come with me." He propelled her into the small cubicle that served both as office and break room, then slammed the door shut. Hands braced on the desk behind him, he confronted her.

"You are never to do anything that will put your life at risk."

"I was comforting a small boy and straightening the covers on his bed. I hardly see how that constitutes a risk."

"You know the rules—avoid undue contact, never become personally involved with the patient."

"He's just a child! A scared little boy."

There was something heroic about the child, something that had pulled on his heartstrings from the very beginning so that he'd had a hard time remaining aloof, but he didn't tell Callie that. Instead, he reigned in his heart, a heart that was suddenly threatening revolt.

"If you wish to remain here as a part of my team, you will follow the rules. Is that understood?"

"Perfectly."

She saluted, a gesture filled with both spunk and humor, but Joseph refused to bend, even a little.

"Your survival depends on total professionalism."

She lifted her chin. "I don't know where you learned your skills, Doctor. But where I come from, professionalism allows for a little compassion."

Head high, back stiff, she marched out. Joseph had to remain behind a few moments to compose himself before he joined her.

He had been unnecessarily harsh with her. He could tell himself it was for her own good, that he'd only been trying to protect her, but he knew better. Joseph was many things, some of them not so attractive, but he was not a liar, not even to himself.

Here was the simple truth: Callie Red Cloud had already gotten under his skin. The thing he had to do was ensure that she didn't get into his heart.

There was a tapping on the door, and Sister Beatrice stuck her head in.

"Dr. Swift, can you come?"

"What is it, Sister?"

"Five new cases just brought in."

Five new cases. He'd hoped the virus might be running its course. If this trend continued, the hospital would soon run out of beds.

Joseph hurried out to face the enemy.

Chapter Four

It was nearly midnight when the exhausted team of virologists crawled into their beds. Callie wanted nothing more than to fall into the oblivion of sleep, however brief, but Peg was wound up and wanted to talk.

"You don't mind, do you?" she asked.

"Of course not." Callie remembered her first day in the field. She'd needed a sounding board, and Jennifer had obliged. She quickly propped an extra pillow under her head and prayed she could keep her eyes open. "Talk, Peg. I'm listening."

"I didn't know it would be like this." The dim glow of the lantern emphasized the dark circles under Peg's eyes. "I don't know what I expected but not this…this dreadful, horrible…" Choking on sobs, she doubled over and buried her face in her hands.

Callie left her bed and put her arms around her friend.

"Cry it out, Peg."

"I'm sorry...I feel so helpless."

"We all do." Callie glanced toward the trailer next door. A faint light still glowed inside, but there was no sign of an occupant. "Even Joseph."

Peg jerked upright, and angrily swiped her face with the back of her hand. "You've got to be kidding. That man has ice water in his veins. I take back every good thing I ever said about him."

"I know he was hard on you, Peg..."

"Hard on me? My lord, Godzilla is kind compared to him. If I ever get out of this godforsaken place I'm going to request that I *never* be sent out with him again."

The problem was far more serious than it seemed. In dealing with a hot agent, teamwork was crucial. Every decision they made had life-or-death consequences. Even the smallest conflict loomed large when the stakes were so high.

"Maybe you should think about calling Ron and asking him to send a replacement, Peg."

"You're telling me to quit? To ditch everything I've worked for?"

"You wouldn't be quitting. You would be making a decision based on what's best for the team."

"Thanks a lot. That sure buoys my self-esteem."

Callie raked her hands through her hair. "I didn't mean that the way it sounded. You're great in the lab, Peg. Brilliant. But some people just aren't cut out for field-work."

"It was my first day, for Pete's sake. Nobody's perfect. Not even you."

Callie didn't respond to the jab, and Peg was immediately contrite.

"I didn't mean that, Callie. It's just nerves."

"Forget it. You're tired and scared. We both are."

"Yeah, I'm scared."

So scared that Peg had frozen up more than once today. Thank goodness Joseph hadn't noticed. If he had, Callie was certain she wouldn't even be having this conversation. Peg Cummings would already be on a plane headed back to Atlanta.

"Then ask for that replacement, Peg. The work we do at the center is just as important as the work we do here in the field. And you have Mike to think about."

"Look, I can make it. I know I can. Just bear with me, okay?"

"I'll do everything I can to help you. But if tomorrow is no better, promise me you'll think about going home."

"I will. Thanks, pal." Peg flashed her dimples. "You look beat. Get some sleep. And don't you dare dream about you know who."

"Not a chance."

Callie didn't dream at all. She waited until Peg was sleeping then stole outside and headed toward the pinpoint of light next door.

Joseph saw her coming, but he didn't didn't reach for shirt and pants, didn't miss a beat. Instead he sat in his boxer shorts strumming his guitar and waiting.

He didn't have long to wait. Callie pulled open the door, then leaned against the jamb, hip slung out.

"Hank Williams?" she said.

" 'I'm So Lonesome I Could Cry.' " Joseph kept strumming.

"I didn't know country-and-western was popular in Italy." He quirked an eyebrow, and she added, "That's where you live, isn't it?"

"Research, or personal interest?"

"I try to know everything about the people I work with,

except the brand of toothpaste, of course. I don't think that matters.''

"Colgate." He strummed a few bars. "What does matter to you, Callie?''

"Music, laughter, hugs. There was a lot of that where I grew up.''

Joseph added that bit of information to his storehouse about Callie. Affection. Music and laughter. She'd come from a happy home.

"May I come in?" she said.

"I'm surprised you asked." He nodded. "Sit down.''

She sat on the bunk opposite his, slender hands folded in her lap, a glimpse of leg visible where her robe fell open. Joseph was acutely aware of her.

"I assume this is not a social visit," he said.

"No.''

She arched her back and raked her fingers through long, dark hair, a glorious panther limbering her muscles, getting ready for the kill.

"I've come to talk to you about Peg.''

"I saw what happened today," Joseph said. Callie widened her eyes. "You need not pretend ignorance. She froze up. More than once, and you stepped into the breach.''

"That's what teamwork is all about.''

"No. That's cover-up work, and I won't allow it. Not on this team. Not in this place. I don't have to tell you that every minute is crucial. Every move we make must count.''

"You're going to send her home?''

"Yes.''

"That's not fair.''

He could see by the set of her jaw that she was going to fight to the bitter end for her friend. Loyalty. He liked that. He liked the way she looked curled on the bed in his room, as if she belonged there, as if she were waiting for a treasured nighttime ritual that would start with a soft kiss and end with the two of them tangled together under the white sheets. He liked the way the lamplight shone in her hair, like stars he could catch by the simple act of running his fingers through her velvet black mane.

There was serenity in the way she held herself, and a dignity that he'd seen in ancient Italian women as they sat in their doorways holding their sewing and watching the world with dark knowing eyes. He guessed the dignity was part of her Apache heritage, but the serenity was all her own.

He liked Callie Red Cloud very much...too much. Her sweet smell seduced him, her beautiful body beckoned to him. He had to put an end to this late-night visit before it was too late, before he was lost.

He flung his guitar aside and stood up so he would tower over her. Tonight he needed every advantage.

"Peg Cummings is not right for the team."

Callie stood toe-to-toe with him, the set of her jaw daring him to try to back her down.

"You're the one who's not right for the team, *Doctor*. You with your arrogant ways and your stone heart. My God, you're a regular Jekyll and Hyde. Saint Peter himself couldn't work with you."

Cheeks flushed, eyes flashing, she paused to compose herself. Joseph was fascinated. Anger enhanced her beauty, heightened her appeal. She reminded him of another dark beauty who had turned his blood to fire.

"You're skating on thin ice, Callie. Watch your step."

"Or what, *Doctor?*" She moved in on him, so close now he could feel the soft chenille of her robe brushing against his chest, and underneath... Ah, what lay underneath her robe defied description. "You'll send me back, too?"

She moved closer, pressing home more than her point. There was ice in her voice and fire in her eyes, a heady combination.

Something savage rose in him, something dark and long buried that was more than need, more than desire. It was passion, primal and earthy, a passion that called storms down from the heavens and flames up from the earth, a passion that shook mountains and moved rivers from their appointed course, a passion so raw and real he knew it was rooted deep in his Sioux heritage.

Retreat, his mind told him. *Charge,* his heart demanded.

For the first time in what seemed forever, Joseph followed his heart.

His kiss shook Callie to the bones. Even as her mind urged her to flee from his embrace, her heart bade her stay. Even as she struggled to hang on to an icy reserve, her body went up in flames.

His was no ordinary kiss, no grazing of lips that left no trace. His was a soul-searing merger that left her dazed and branded.

How could this be? How was it she had come to his trailer to discuss something so important that lives hung in the balance, and ended up in his arms, with no thought in her head except to savor this intense pleasure, to give in to the primal urges that raged through her?

She swayed into him, melding their bodies with a shamelessness that would have been shocking had it not seemed so right.

He was wrong for her. She knew this to be true. But Callie was also Apache, and her native upbringing had taught her how to live in the moment, how to *be.*

She would accept his kiss without regret, savor the moment without thought for tomorrow, for somewhere deep inside Callie knew that the man who kissed her was not Joseph Swift, the practical doctor, but Swift Hawk, the passionate Sioux. Perhaps it was the night, hot and sultry, or perhaps it was the moon, a golden bowl riding the clouds in a darkened sky. But whatever the source, Callie knew that it was dangerous to question magic.

"Never question gifts from the Great Spirit," her Apache grandmother used to tell her.

"What would happen?" Even as a child Callie had wanted to know the *why* of everything.

"The universe gives and it takes away."

"How?"

"Go play with your dolls, Callie. I have no time for little girls who are like naughty squirrels, always chasing their tails and never storing their nuts."

Callie lost her breath, and still Joseph held her captive in his arms—a willing captive. A love poem her father had written to her mother came to mind, a poem on yellowing paper stored away in a scrapbook.

Strong winds blow round us.
Storms rage as we embrace,
   but nothing can separate us,
   for the roots of your heart
   entangle with mine.
The sweet juice of your sugar tree
   runs through my veins,
And we are one.

Something deep inside Callie cried out, her heart and soul searching for the beauty and the music of love. For one moment in Joseph's arms, she caught a glimpse of how it could be, of how it would feel, and then her mind took over and the practical Callie shut herself off to all possibilities.

Whether Joseph sensed the change in her or whether she made a sound, she would never know what ended the kiss. All she knew is that suddenly she was standing apart from him, arms wrapped around herself as if she could hold his warmth next to her skin forever.

"You must think me brazen," she said.

"No."

That was all he would give her, one word, but it was enough. Callie's dignity settled over her like a mantle, and she studied her adversary, head up, chin out.

"I didn't come here tonight for this," she said.

Was that a fleeting smile she saw or something else, a small movement at the corners of his mouth that might be pain?

"I came to plead, not so much for Peg Cummings, but for all of us—you, me, Peg. Something is amiss, but I still think we can work as a team. The answer is not to send her away, but to come to terms with each other, to declare a truce of sorts."

"You speak eloquently."

"Thank you. My grandmother told me to always speak straight so my words would go as sunlight into the heart."

Joseph retreated deep into himself, thinking. Callie allowed him his silence, for thought comes before speech and in silence dwells truth. Another bit of wisdom she'd learned at the knee of her Apache grandmother.

"I will make my peace with Peg," Joseph finally said.

"Thank you."

"And with you..."

He was as still as a rock, a tree, offering neither gesture

nor facial expression to betray his deepest feelings. If he had any.

"...but first I must know why you hold me in such contempt."

"I don't..." His eyes pierced through her lie, and Callie told him the truth. "I am proud of being half Apache, but you deny your Native American heritage."

"I have my reasons."

He shut himself up then, deep as a river, and Callie nodded, showing her acceptance.

She left his trailer quickly. Strains of guitar music followed her into the darkness and all the way to the door of her temporary home—"Unforgettable," each note vibrating with emotion as if it were plucked straight from the musician's soul.

Chapter Five

You deny your Native American heritage....

Joseph continued strumming while Callie's words rang
through his mind. He had not thought about his father in
many years, and now bewitched by this lovely Apache
sorceress he could no longer shut out his history.

It wasn't a pretty one. The only heroic thing his father
ever did was die. He'd been shot down in the jungles of
Vietnam and was buried with honors at Arlington.

Joseph had stayed behind with his grandmother while
his mother flew into D.C. for the funeral. He'd never seen
the grave and didn't plan to. Let sleeping dogs lie, that
was his philosophy.

It hadn't always been that way. Once he'd thought
Rocky Swift Hawk was the greatest man alive. His mother
told him it was so. She had the war medals to prove it,
and before that the certificates of honor from high school,
college, then later medical school.

That's where they'd met, Sarah Brave Crow and Rocky Swift Hawk, both studious, both good-looking and both Sioux.

Joseph had grown up wanting to be exactly like his father.

"He was the most brilliant man in medical school," Sarah had told him. "A natural healer. Everybody knew he would be great. What they didn't know is that part of his greatness was because of this."

She'd gone to the cedar chest, brought out a small deer-skin bag, then placed it carefully into Joseph's hands.

"This is your father's sacred bundle." She untied the bag and took out a single feather, brown with reddish tips. "The swift hawk came to him in spirit dreams. It was his talisman, Joseph, the source of his strength."

There were other objects inside the bag—a small smooth rock, a seashell, an elk's tooth, a single blue crystal—all from spirit dreams, all symbolic.

In the Sioux tradition, Sarah held a ceremony to officially transfer the bag and all its power to Joseph.

He'd been twelve at the time. When he was thirteen he started hating his father.

Joseph laid his guitar on the bed, then pulled opened one of the cabinets in the trailer and took out his father's sacred bundle. He held it in his hand for a long time, thoughtful.

He'd learned the ugly truth at school.

"Joseph Swift Hawk thinks he's such hot stuff, getting all A's. He's nothing but a bastard."

"How do you know?"

"My daddy said so, said his old man got drunk at a party in med school and raped his mother, then wouldn't marry her."

"That's a lie!" Joseph charged towards the two boys

he'd overheard on the playground, both fists flashing. He'd been suspended from school for fighting, but not before he inflicted severe damage to Ray Black Dog and Jim Little Pipe. Both had black eyes, and Ray had a chipped front tooth.

At home, Joseph confronted his mother.

"I want to know the truth," he said.

And so she'd told him how Rocky had always been the most handsome, the most brilliant man she'd ever met…and the most flawed. He had a penchant for strong drink and hot words. At a Christmas party he'd been drunk and fighting. Sarah rescued him, took him out into the night to get some fresh air. He took the friendship she offered, and more.

"I could have stopped him, but even drunk he was the most wonderful man I'd ever known, the most wonderful man I could imagine knowing. And so I didn't protest.

"Later, when I discovered I was pregnant, he offered to marry me, but I knew Rocky. With a wife and child to support, he would never have stayed in school and the world would have been deprived of a great doctor. And so I chose to raise you alone."

Joseph's fist closed around the skin bag, then he flung it into the cabinet and slammed the door. No decent man would allow the woman who carried his child to go into the world alone. No self-respecting man would deny his son.

From that day, Joseph turned his back on everything Sioux, including his name. He went into medicine, not because of his father, but because of his mother. She'd sacrificed a degree for him and so he earned one for her, and for himself. As Dr. Swift he moved far beyond his Sioux heritage, so far that when he met Maria it was easy to embrace not only her family but her country as well.

Never until tonight had Joseph wondered if he'd done the right thing. Never until Callie challenged him had he questioned his motives.

He fell asleep wondering how and why she had bewitched him.

The minute Callie woke she knew everything had changed.

Never again could she look at Joseph Swift Hawk in the same way. Not after their late-night conversation. Not after the kiss.

She groaned and wrapped the covers tighter around herself. She didn't want to get up, didn't want to see him.

"Callie?" Peg shook her shoulder. "Are you all right?"

"Yes. What time is it?"

"Time to make breakfast. It's your turn, remember?"

At least it would give her something to do besides sit across the table from Joseph sipping coffee and pretend nothing had happened.

There was a knock on the door. "Peg, I need to talk to you."

"Speak of the devil," Callie muttered.

"I couldn't have put it better myself." Peg raked a brush through her hair. "Be right there, Dr. Swift," she called to him, then turned to Callie. "What do you suppose that ogre wants?"

"He wants to smoke the peace pipe."

"How do you know?"

"Mind reading. Old Apache trick." Callie threw back the covers then shoved Peg gently toward the door. "Go on out there and use your charm. I'll bet you'll discover that he's more than willing to meet you halfway."

She caught a fleeting glimpse of Joseph when Peg went

out the door, but that was all it took. She felt a sweet rush through her body, and had to sit back down on the bed to recover. Callie Red Cloud was not the swooning kind, and yet here she was, languishing away.

That couldn't be tenderness she was feeling, could it? That couldn't be longing.

Callie Red Cloud was not the longing type. Instead, she hurried to the kitchen and made quick work of breakfast.

By the time Joseph and Peg joined her, she had stacks of pancakes dripping in butter, a huge pile of bacon, crisped exactly the way she liked it, and a pot of strong black coffee.

Peg was smiling, and even Joseph seemed to be in a jocular mood.

"What did you two talk about?" Callie asked Peg as they were suiting up. Though she knew the subject, she wanted all the details. Her brother used to laugh and call her Miss Inquisitive.

"Callie, don't you know curiosity killed the cat?"

"I'll take my chances."

"You're incorrigible."

"And you're avoiding the subject."

"Right."

"Does this mean you're not going to tell me, or does it mean you want me to grovel and beg?"

"Grovel and beg."

"Never. I'm not the groveling kind."

Their good-natured bantering lasted until they went out into the sunshine for inspection, their arms around each other, laughing. Peg had a high ringing laugh, like bells, but Callie's was full-bodied and deep-throated.

Joseph watched and waited, letting Callie's laughter wash over him in sweet waves. It was cathartic, healing, exactly the antidote he needed before facing the task that lay ahead.

"Ready for inspection, Doctor," Callie said.

Her usual disdain was missing…or was it merely wishful thinking on his part?

He inspected Peg first, and as she passed the barrier into the quarantined area he turned to Callie.

"I've saved the best for last," he said, surprising both of them.

"Am I the best?"

Their eyes met, held, and she replayed their kiss in her mind a thousand times before he could answer her.

"Yes," he said, all hint of levity vanished, "you're the best."

As they passed the barrier and walked toward the hospital every nerve in her body tingled with awareness of him. It was a great relief to Callie when Sister Mary Margaret rushed through the door to meet them.

"Dr. Swift, we have the most marvelous news. Little Ricardo is sitting up, demanding food. Tacos, of all things."

Little Ricardo was not sitting on his bed: he was bouncing. Sister Beatrice flapped around him like a great black bird while Sister Mary Margaret covered her mouth like a schoolgirl to hold back her giggles.

Joseph sat beside the small boy, conversing in perfect Spanish while he checked all his vital signs.

"So, you want tacos?"

"Yes, with green chilies."

"Are you planning to start a fire somewhere?" Joseph patted the small boy's stomach. "Perhaps in here?"

The child's laughter pealed through the hospital, and patients who hadn't heard the sound in days smiled.

"First, let's see what we can do about getting you a good bath and some clothes. Sister Beatrice?"

She gathered Ricardo in her voluminous embrace, and as they walked away nothing could be seen of him except the top of his dark head and legs as thin as matchsticks. Joseph stared after them, deep in thought.

"The doctor has a heart after all," Callie said, softly.

"Did you think otherwise?"

"Yes."

"Even after last night?"

Callie couldn't meet his eyes, couldn't answer his question. Instead, she changed the subject.

"How soon can he go home?"

"He has no home. His parents died in the first wave of the outbreak."

"What about his other relatives?"

"All gone. Little Ricardo Valesquez has no one...except us."

There was tenderness in Joseph's face when he spoke of the child, a gentleness Callie had not seen. And his voice was so intimate when he said *us* that Callie thought he meant the two of them. Together. A team, and so much more.

She would have asked him what he meant, but he was already striding away, taking care of other patients.

"Best if I do my own work instead of mulling over him," she muttered.

"Mulling over who?" Peg handed Callie a handful of charts.

"Nobody."

"Would that be the same nobody who handled little Ricky as if he had a houseful of his own children?"

"Ricky?"

''He told Beatrice that's what he wants to be called, and you didn't answer my nosy question.''

''Do you suppose he plans to make the tacos himself?''

''Who?''

''Nobody.'' Callie grinned. ''Let's get to work.''

Chapter Six

Joseph had the tacos delivered to his trailer that night for dinner, and the doctors and nurses who could be spared as well as the team of virologists shared Ricky's celebration meal.

Ricky sat between Callie and Peg, and both women doted on him. As it turned out, he spoke English most of the time, but when he was excited he always turned to the more expressive language of his parents.

"What did he say?" Peg asked. "Something about the ground?"

Callie laughed. *"Grande.* Big. He's telling you how big his belly is." She leaned over to pat Ricky's tummy, then she patted her own flat stomach. "Mine, too. I think I ate too much. I'm on fire."

She looked straight at Joseph, and what she saw in his eyes excited her beyond imagination. The same fire burned in them both, and it had nothing to do with tacos.

She couldn't tear her eyes away from his, and she wondered if the others noticed.

Fortunately, Ricky saved her. "Tell me a story," he said, tugging at her hand.

"All right. How about a fairy tale?"

"No." He cocked his head and stared at her. "Are you a real Indian?"

"Yes, I am." She sought Joseph, and found him studying her. "My mother is from Mississippi, but my father is a full-blooded Apache. That makes me a true Native American."

The child didn't need such a detailed explanation. Was she throwing another challenge at Joseph?

"Tell him the legend of the prairie rose," Joseph said.

"Yeah," Ricky said.

"My mother told it to me when I was a child. It was always a favorite of mine," Joseph said.

"Tell it, Callie. Tell it." Ricky climbed into her lap and laid his head on her chest. Time moved backward and Callie was sitting before a campfire deep in the heart of the White Mountains, her head on her father's chest while he told the legend of the rose. It was prairie lore, originating with the Dakota-Sioux.

That Joseph had declared it his favorite was almost the same as declaring himself Sioux.

"Long ago when the world was young and Mother Earth was just a girl," Callie began, "the prairie had no flowers, only green grasses and brown shrubs, for nothing else could withstand the fierce breath of the Wind Demon."

Her voice was lyrical, its musical cadences rising and falling as she told how the flowers came up from Mother Earth's heart, one by one, only to be destroyed by the Wind Demon. Something inside Joseph trembled, melted, and he found himself longing for his childhood, for a time when he was certain of the goodness of the world and the honor of his father. For the first time in many years, his heart yearned, and he felt a glimmer of hope, not merely for himself, but for Callie, for Ricky, for all of mankind.

"And then the sweet shy prairie rose asked permission of Mother Earth to go to the prairie."

Ricky was almost asleep, and Callie brushed his hair back from his forehead. The tenderness of the gesture tore at Joseph's heart.

"And when the Demon Wind smelled the sweet fragrance of prairie rose his heart melted and he abandoned his fierce ways to became a kind and gentle breeze."

Ricky was asleep in her lap. One by one the valiant warriors stole from the kitchen and went to bed so they would be prepared to do battle the next day.

Only Joseph and Callie were left, with Ricky cuddled against her breast. They didn't speak for a long time, but instead sat in quiet communion with the magic of the story still between them.

"What will we do with him?" Callie said.

"For now, he stays with me. Does that surprise you so?"

"Am I that easy to read?"

"Not always, but sometimes. Last night, for instance."

He was sitting across the table from her, not touching, and yet Callie felt his yearning. She tried to shut the door against him, but she was powerless.

She formed her mouth to make a denial, but nothing came out.

"You make me want too much, Callie."

"I don't think I want to hear any more of this, Joseph."

"Your lips say no, but your eyes speak the truth."

"Tonight when you admitted that the legend of the rose

is your favorite story, were you also admitting your Sioux heritage?''

"Is that so important to you?"

"Yes."

"I don't know, Callie. Perhaps my heart was admitting the truth, but in my mind there is still a question."

She nodded. It wasn't what she'd hoped to hear, but for now it was enough.

She shifted the sleeping child. "Who will tell him about his parents?"

"I've already told him."

"How did he react?"

"He has a child's natural resilience as well as a child's natural optimism… How do we lose that, Callie?"

"Reality forced upon us, I suppose. All the magic pushed out…I don't know."

"Do you know what he said?" Joseph came around the table and put his hand on the child's head. "He said, 'Who will be my mommy?'"

Tears stung Callie's eyes, and she made no attempt to hide them. Joseph knelt beside her and caught the teardrops with the tips of his fingers, then he cupped her face, softly, tenderly, in the way of a man who loves a woman.

"If I were any other man I would fall in love with you, Callie. I would fight demons and slay dragons to keep the tears from your eyes."

He caressed her cheeks until the tears stopped, then he kissed her softly on the lips, lifted the child from her arms and left her alone in the kitchen.

"But you're not another man," she whispered. "And I'm not another woman. You are Wind Demon and I can never be Shy Prairie Rose."

Joseph tucked the child into bed, then kissed his downy cheek, turned off the lights and climbed into his own bed.

A full moon rode the Texas sky, and in the pale light Joseph could see the small hump under the covers, a little bundle hardly bigger than a knapsack. He got up to check Ricky's pulse and respiration, then stood for a while watching the slow rise and fall of his breathing. It was like having a child of his own.

Almost.

Ricky awoke crying in the middle of the night, crying for his mother.

"I'm here." Joseph gathered the little boy in his arms and sat on the edge of the bed, rocking. "Everything's going to be all right, Ricky. I'm here."

Ricky wadded Joseph's undershirt in his fists and cried even harder.

"How about a glass of warm milk?" Ricky's answer was a fresh outburst. "How about a cookie? Does that sound great, pal?"

"I want my mommy." Ricky went into a fresh gale of weeping.

Joseph walked the floor with him, he sang, he cajoled. But nothing could calm the child.

In desperation Joseph wrapped a blanket around both of them, Indian style, and stepped out into the night. A sliver of moon and stars sprinkled sparsely across the sky shed a surreal light, so that when Callie stepped out of her trailer she looked like a spirit, the legendary ghost woman of the Tetons who had stolen the heart of a Sioux brave.

She didn't see them at first, for they were standing in the shadow of the trailer. Joseph took advantage of this camouflage to savor her, the golden skin turned luminescent by the moon, the tumble of hair like a waterfall, the exquisite face with cheeks like knife blades and lips made for kissing.

Selfish. He was selfish to the core for taking his fill of her while the child was in need.

"Callie, over here."

In the darkness she seemed to drift toward them, a cloud, a spirit, a dream.

"I heard him crying," she said.

"I'm sorry it woke you."

"I wasn't sleeping well anyhow."

She was beside them now, and Joseph did the most natural thing in the world: he opened the blanket and she came inside. She wrapped her arms around the child, Joseph wrapped his arms around her, and the three of them stood cocooned by the blanket while the moon tracked across the sky.

Words weren't necessary. Sheltered by love and compassion, Ricky grew quiet and finally fell asleep. And still Callie and Joseph stayed as they were, holding on to each other, an island unto themselves, safe under the blanket.

Her nightgown was white cotton and prim. But there was nothing prim about the body underneath. The imprint of her branded Joseph. Heart pounding like native drums, he memorized the curve of her hip and the shape of her breasts. In the pale moonlight he saw how the hollow at the base of a woman's throat could drive a man mad with longing. He felt how the silkiness of a woman's hair could inspire a man to write poetry. He understood how the touch of a woman's soft skin could move a man to sing songs of love.

She stirred against him, sighing. "I suppose I should go."

"Not yet."

"Ricky's sleeping."

"He might wake up and need you."

"I didn't do anything, not really."

"You held him, Callie." He shifted Ricky onto one shoulder so her could draw Callie closer. "Sometimes that's enough."

She wrapped her arms tightly around his waist.

"Yes," she said. "Sometimes it is."

Tension began to build along Joseph's spine, and his body heat increased a hundredfold. What had started as a warm embrace rapidly turned into burning need. Callie's response was instantaneous. She became liquid in his arms.

He bent down and caught her lower lip between his teeth, teasing the tender flesh, sucking, nipping. Her mouth flowered open for him, and he braced his back against the trailer under the impact of their kiss.

He shifted. She moved. They swayed, hips perfectly melded, feeling each other through their clothes and wanting more, ever so much more.

The child was featherlight in his arms, and the blanket gave them privacy, shelter from the awful storm that raged a few feet away, just beyond the barriers.

Joseph knew he was courting danger, knew he had to put a stop to this madness, but not yet. Not yet.

He explored the soft inner recesses of her mouth with his tongue, taking her sweet nectar for himself. Need rode him hard, and his exploration became bolder, his tongue an extension of himself, a driving force that sought to be satisfied.

Callie was liquid heat, a dark mystery in his arms, a sweet hot miracle, and he knew if he held on too long he wouldn't be able to let her go. Not now. Not ever.

The aching void opened within him even before he released her. She tightened her grip on him, sensing his turmoil, and then she let go. Her chest rose and fell rapidly with her breathing, and he felt as if his heart would burst.

"Sometimes holding is not enough," he said.

"No. Sometimes it only makes us long for things we know we can't have."

She pressed her forehead into the hollow of his throat, and he kissed the top of her head.

"Callie, you are the most appealing woman I've ever met."

She waited. He loved that about her, the dignified stillness that gave a man space to move and speak freely.

"I lost one woman I loved to the *arbo* virus. I won't risk that again."

She cupped his cheeks, kissed him softly on the lips, then lifted the edge of the blanket to steal away into the night. Something shifted inside Joseph, ideas rearranging themselves, reason abdicating to heart.

"Callie...stay."

Chapter Seven

It was all so simple really. Joseph said "stay," and once again Callie followed her heart instead of her mind.

In the morning she would tell Peg she'd stayed because of the child, but she knew that wasn't so. She'd stay for one reason and one reason only: in a bed not two feet away, Joseph Swift Hawk lay sleeping, one arm flung above his head and the other crossed over his chest.

Moonlight coming through the window illuminated his profile, and she lay on her side with Ricky cuddled close, studying the man who turned her inside out.

"I'll sleep here, you'll be there, in case Ricky wakes."

That's what Joseph had said when they went inside his trailer. That and nothing more.

He'd made no attempt to kiss her again, no move to indicate that he had anything on his mind except the well-being of the child.

Noble and proper. That's how Callie would view her

current sleeping arrangement if she weren't so honest. But she'd never lied to anybody, especially herself, and she wasn't about to start now.

Certainly she wanted to be there for Ricky. But she was in Joseph's trailer because she wanted to be with him. Even if she couldn't be in his bed, she could be close enough to watch him sleep, to listen to him breathe.

Even to touch him if she wanted to.

Her hand stole from under the covers, reached across the way. And suddenly his was there, closing around hers, fingers linked, palms pressed close.

"I thought you were sleeping," she said.

"No. Dreaming."

He rolled onto his side facing her, and their hands swung in the space between the beds.

"We've made a bridge," she said.

"I hope so."

Ricky stirred, burrowing his little body closer to hers. She'd never thought of herself as maternal, but with the sleeping child next to her, she felt a kinship to mothers everywhere.

"What will happen to Ricky?" she said.

"Foster homes, probably."

"I can't bear to think of that."

"As long as this area is quarantined, nothing will change."

She tried to read his face in the silence, but there wasn't enough light. He was wrong, of course. From the moment she came into his trailer, everything changed.

No matter how they viewed their relationship, their colleagues would take the obvious view: they were lovers.

Joseph had to know that: he was too smart not to. Personally she didn't care what anybody thought or said about her as long as she was comfortable with herself.

"Callie, I'm glad you came out when you heard the child crying."

"Ricky wasn't the only reason I came out."

"He wasn't the only reason I asked you to stay."

"I know."

"If you weren't over there, and he weren't beside you..." Joseph squeezed her hand. "So many ifs."

"Good night, Joseph. Sweet dreams."

"You can count on it, Callie."

Ricky was the first one awake. He sat up in bed, looked at the two doctors, and decided on the spot to adopt them. He climbed out of bed, stood exactly between their beds and gave them the first hint.

"Mommy and Daddy always kissed me good morning."

He made his announcement in his loudest voice, and in very good English so they would understand. He laughed when they both sat up.

"Callie first," Ricky said.

She hugged him when she kissed, and he liked that. She smelled nice, and he liked that, too. She kissed him and patted his head and kissed him again. She was pretty when she laughed.

The doctor was sitting on the bed watching them, and Ricky hadn't decided exactly what to call him.

"I'm stealing all his sugar, Joseph. You'd better come and get yours before it's all gone."

Ricky decided to call him Joe.

"What's *stealing sugar,* Joe?"

"It's another name for kissing, probably learned from her Mississippi relatives. Why don't you ask Callie the origin."

"What's orchin?"

"You started all this, Joe. I'm going to leave it with you while I go and roust Peg out of bed. Bye, sugar, I'll see you later." She waved to them at the door.

"Okay," Joe said teasingly.

"I was speaking to Ricky."

"You wound me."

Callie put her hand on Joe's forehead, then took his wrist and counted his pulse, just like she did in the hospital except it never took so long when she did it for Ricky.

"You'll live," she said.

"Yes, but will I be happy?"

"Time will tell," she said.

After Callie left, Joe told him all about *origin* and *beginnings* and *roots* that had nothing to with stuff you planted in the garden, and for a little while Ricky forgot that he would never see his mommy and daddy again.

He had to stay with Sister Beatrice that day, and she was all right. She taught him a new song about six little ducks and told him stories about the three bears and a little girl called Goldilocks, but he liked Callie's stories best.

Tonight he was going to ask her to tell another story, and then he was going to cuddle up close to her so he wouldn't have bad dreams.

When it got dark he had dinner with Sister Beatrice and then she told him it was time for bed.

"Where's Joe?" he asked.

"He's still at the hospital. Don't worry. I'll stay right here until he gets back."

She hugged him and he nearly smothered under her long robes. His mother had told him they were called habits, and then he wondered if they were bad habits. She was so pretty when she laughed, and then she'd explained

how a nun's habit was different from a bad habit like
going to bed without saying your prayers.

"Can I wait to say my prayers until Joe and Callie
come?" he asked.

"Callie won't be coming here, only Doctor Swift," she
said, but Ricky knew better. "I think it's best if you say
your prayers before you go to sleep."

"Okay." Ricky knelt beside his bed and asked God to
bless everybody he knew except Sister Beatrice who
didn't tell good stories.

Then he climbed into bed and shut his eyes, but he
wasn't about to go to sleep. He was saving his real prayers
for when Joe and Callie came home.

Joseph knelt beside the sleeping child to take his pulse.
At least that's what he'd intended, but something happened when he got close. He was no longer a doctor caring for a patient: he was a man filled with tenderness and
longing, tenderness for the small homeless boy and longing for things he'd told himself he could never have—a
wife, a child, a family of his own.

He put his hand on the little forehead, and was relieved
when it felt cool. Then he lifted the tiny hand and studied
the little network of veins, the smooth brown skin, the
plump fingers, and he was filled with wonder.

Such a miracle, a child. Such a perfect little being.
What were his hopes, his dreams? How would life shape
him?

Joseph would never know. As soon as his job here was
over, he'd move on to the next one, and the next. On and
on until he was a very old man, if the fates were kind and
the Great Spirit smiled on him.

Old and alone.

Impatiently he shut out his thoughts, checked his watch and started counting the heartbeats.

"Joe?" Ricky sat up, rubbing his eyes and looking around. "Where's Callie?"

"In her trailer with Peg."

"I want Callie."

"I do, too, but it's bedtime, pal. Time for you to go back to sleep."

"I saved my prayers for you and Callie."

"Okay, pal, let's hear them."

"No, not till Callie comes."

Joseph had no experience dealing with children. He was an only child, and after Maria died he avoided being around other people's children. Ben had tried to draw him into his family life a couple of times—invited him to ball games and birthday parties—but Joseph always remained aloof.

Now he wished he'd taken Ben up on his offers. Here was a sleepy, querulous child—who had suffered loss that would fell most adults—making a simple request.

The one request Joseph had to deny.

"Listen, she's worked very hard today and she'll have to work very hard until all those people in the hospital are well."

Or dead. Joseph shook his head to clear it.

"She needs her sleep, and so do you."

"I have to pray before I sleep or I'll die and go to hell." Ricky puckered up. "I want Callie."

Joseph had seen the way Sister Beatrice looked at him when he came home. The damage was already done. What would one more night in his trailer matter?

With that, he made his way to Callie's trailer.

"Callie, I need you."

Joseph's voice penetrated her sleep, and Callie was instantly alert. Almost as if she'd been waiting for him.

She flung aside the covers and slipped out the door. There he was, standing in the moonlight with a blanket wrapped around himself, a blanket with a hump that could be none other than little Ricky.

Callie had a hard time making her heart behave. Of course he was there because of the child, but he'd said, *I need you.*

I need you too, Joseph, she thought, but she wasn't about to say the words aloud. She was too smart. Darkness brings out our fears as well as our dreams, her grandmother had told her, and now she was facing both, for Joseph was both dream and fear.

"I'll come," she said, and he nodded, then strode ahead of her toward his trailer.

The minute she stepped inside, the rest of the world vanished. Nothing existed for her except this child, this man and this moment.

"I didn't want to wake you, Callie, but this is an emergency."

Alarmed, she looked at the small boy cradled against Joseph's shoulder. "What's wrong?"

"Ricky's crisis is not physical, it's spiritual. He says he can't say prayers without you, and if he doesn't say his prayers he's in mortal fear of eternal damnation."

Callie suppressed a smile, and Ricky leaned back so he could look at Joseph.

"What's infernal dalmation?"

"This is going to be a long night." Joseph's gaze swept Callie from tip to toe. "A very long night."

Heat rose in Callie, and she pushed her heavy hair back from her flushed face.

"We'll talk about all that tomorrow, Ricky," she said.

"Let's hear those prayers so we can all get a good night's sleep."

Joseph set Ricky in the middle of the bed, but he barreled out then faced them, hands on his hips.

"We have to all hold hands," he announced.

"Like this?" Callie caught one hand and Joseph the other.

"No. In a circle."

When Joseph caught her hand, she felt the shock all the way to her toes. Even the roots of her hair tingled.

"God, it's me—Ricky—and my new mommy and daddy."

A little boy blurted out his dream, and Callie squeezed Joseph's hand so hard her knuckles turned white. Oh, God, what were they going to do?

"Bless the sick people and make them well. Bless the nuns...Sister Beatrice, too, and help her learn good stories."

The little hand squeezed hard, and Callie thought his prayers were over.

"God, I saved the best for last," Ricky whispered "Bless Joe and Callie best in the world. Amen."

Ricky was asleep by the time they'd tucked the covers under his chin. Callie turned to Joseph to ask the question burning in her mind, but one look at him, and her words died.

He cupped her face, then tangled his hands in her long hair and gently drew her toward him. Her white gown brushed against his thighs. The heat of him seared her, even through the cotton material.

"I can't look at you without wanting you," he whispered. "All of you."

She was tempted beyond imagining. How was she going to endure the night?

"This is neither the time nor the place, Joe."

His grip tightened and he tugged her so close her breasts were flattened against his chest. Desire raged through her so hot and heavy she swayed. Joseph slid his hands downward shaping her slender neck, her narrow shoulders.

Callie held her breath, fighting temptation. But for the child beside them, she would be lost.

His fingers were on her buttons, then on her skin, hot as they moved across her throat, burning as they shaped the mounds of her breasts, searing as they massaged her nipples.

She had died and was in heaven. There was nothing in the world except stars, brilliant as they exploded around her, and the man, the passionate, primal man.

He lowered his head and took her nipples, first one and then the other. His mouth was magic, his tongue, fire.

Callie melted, her insides writhing and twisting. She wove her hands through his hair, pulling him closer, murmuring soft words of encouragement.

Nothing could stop them now. Nothing. Not even the child sleeping in the bed beside them.

She whispered his name, followed by a soft plea. For mercy? For more?

She was beyond knowing, beyond caring.

He knelt in front of her and buried his face in the soft folds of her gown. She felt his breath on her belly, and it turned her to flame.

"Oh, Callie, you make me want so much."

"I know, I know."

She knelt in front of him and they held each other close, foreheads touching, swaying like reeds caught in the wind. From the bed came the soft sounds of the sleeping child.

"You are right, Callie. This is neither the time nor the place."

He pulled her to her feet and pressed his lips to her forehead.

"Ricky needs you. If you're willing to risk the censure, I'd like you to continue staying with us," he said.

"I've already taken the risk, and I don't give a rat's behind about what other people say. Of course, I'll continue coming...for the child's sake."

"This won't happen again. I promise." He didn't have to elaborate. She knew what he was talking about. "Good night, Callie. Sleep well."

She doubted if she would sleep at all. Easing back the covers, she crept in beside Ricky and took comfort from his small warm body. A cloud passed over the moon, and she could see nothing of Joseph except a mound in the darkness.

Would there ever be a time and a place for them?

Chapter Eight

"What do you two do over there every night?" Peg asked.

She and Callie were in the tiny office on one of their rare breaks from caring for the sick. Ordinarily Callie would ignore a question that personal, but Peg was motivated by concern, not curiosity.

"We don't do anything except take care of Ricky. Poor little kid." It was true: she and Joseph hadn't touched since that night Ricky prayed that they would become his parents.

The strain was telling on Callie. She was exhausted, physically and emotionally. She propped her feet on a stool and leaned her head against the back of the chair.

"Do you ever think about having children, Peg?"

"Yes. All the time. Mike wants to start our family now."

"And you?"

"Part of me does, part of me wants this." Peg swept spread her arms to encompass the makeshift hospital, the sophisticated equipment, the safety suit. "This work is so exciting. I can't imagine giving it up."

"Why not have both?"

Peg snorted. "Are you kidding?"

Callie smiled as if to say, of course, I'm kidding. The truth was, she'd been thinking about that for days now, about having both a child and a career.

Not for Peg, though. For herself.

Every day she grew more attached to Ricky. He was smart and funny and he had a way of attaching himself to her heart that made it impossible to think of a future without him. She was thinking of adopting him.

She had told no one, not even Joseph. What would he say? What would he do?

Nothing, probably. He was part of her heart, but he wasn't part of her plans. Both of them were very clear on that.

Callie was opting for single parenthood. Why not? It was happening more and more: career women who didn't want the commitment of marriage but wanted the satisfaction of motherhood were adopting children.

"Speaking of Mike," Peg said. "How soon do you think this will be over?"

"It's hard to say...."

A loud commotion outside stopped Callie.

"I demand answers! The whole city demands answers!"

Callie and Peg rushed to the door in time to see a reporter in boots, gloves, mask and makeshift safety suit confronting Dr. Joseph Swift.

"Out!" Joseph yelled. "Out!"

"The public has a right to know what's happening here."

Icicles were cozy compared to the stare Joseph gave the reporter.

"The fool," Peg muttered. "Doesn't he know what he's stepped into?"

"That's just the problem," Callie said. "I think he does."

Instead of retreating, the reporter advanced.

"My lord, look at that. He's got more courage than brains." Peg opened the door, but Callie pulled her back.

"Wait. We can't risk being cornered and questioned."

As they watched, Joseph turned on his heel and stalked off. Within seconds guards were strong-arming the reporter out the door, through the empty lot and over the barricades.

"Now what?" said Peg.

"Now we return to work. Joseph will handle this."

There were three TV sets in the mayor's office, and every one of them was tuned to the six o'clock news where Dr. Joseph Swift was the lead story.

Grim-faced and sober, Mayor Jim Dillard and Joseph sat on two padded leather chairs listening.

Mac Sanford, the reporter who had breached security at the hospital, led the way.

"The big question tonight is, what's going on in Houston's east side? There's a hospital over there—behind barricades—full of the sick and the dying. And presiding over it all is the world's top virologist, Dr. Joseph Swift of the National Institute of Virology."

The mayor's face whitened. "He's done his homework," he muttered.

The cameras panned in for a close-up of Mac Sanford.

"Virology is the study of viruses, and when I found Dr. Joseph Swift he was wearing a safety suit. So was everybody in that well-guarded, secret hospital.

"Guards, safety suits, barricades. That can mean only one thing. Somewhere deep in the bowels of Houston lurks a hot virus, one so deadly it can wipe out our entire city."

"My God," the mayor said. "How could that leak have happened?"

"It *did* happen," Joseph told him. "We have to decide how we're going to handle it."

Even before the mayor spoke, his phone began to ring. Ignoring it, Jim poured two glasses of wine, handed one to Joseph, then sat behind his desk, silent and pensive.

When he finally spoke he proved why he was one of the most respected mayors Houston had ever had.

"We can't just go out and do damage control. The people deserve more than that." Jim made a tent of his fingers and looked at Joseph. "What is the status of things over there?"

"No new cases in a week. Ten recoveries, twenty deaths, sixteen holding on."

"Is the end in sight?"

"I think so."

"I hope and pray so. Can I truthfully assure my people that the crisis is over?"

One of the predictable things about hot viruses was their unpredictability. No one could say precisely when an episode would end. There were too many unknowns, particularly in a large metropolitan area where people traveled constantly and quickly—going to work, to malls, to theaters, to churches, to sporting events, to concerts, to restaurants.

And yet, Joseph knew the importance of the news

broadcasts. The phone in the mayor's office had not ceased ringing since Mac Sanford dropped his verbal bomb.

"No," Joseph said.

The mayor hung his head and rubbed his temples, then squared his shoulders and walked to the huge bank of windows overlooking the city. There were lights as far as the eye could see.

"Look out there. Three million people in this city. If that many people panic, we might as well light a torch to Houston then sit back and watch it burn." He went back to his desk. "Dr. Swift, what are we going to do?"

What they had to do was very clear to Joseph, the one thing he tried to avoid at all costs.

"I have a plan," he said.

The mayor was pacing, Peg was wringing her hands, and Joseph was having second thoughts. Around them a crew from WCBH set up television cameras while Mac Sanford bent over his notebook rapidly scrawling questions.

The mayor's secretary had been called in for the late-night broadcast, and she was dispensing coffee and calm in equal doses.

"Are you sure you want me to do this?" Peg asked Joseph. "Callie is much more experienced than I am."

"Callie has the experience, I have the experience. But we also have a foreign look, and Americans sometimes don't trust foreigners." Joseph turned Peg toward a mirror over an antique washstand.

"Look at yourself, Peg. You're a vivacious blond, all-American housewife. Never mind that you're also a virologist. You look familiar to them, like their next-door neighbor, the preacher's wife, their son's schoolteacher. You're somebody the people can trust."

"I think I'm going to throw up."

"Not on camera." Joseph patted her shoulder. "You'll do fine, Peg."

"But what if I don't know the answers to the questions he's bound to ask questions?"

"Just be reassuring. That's all we ask."

In Joseph's trailer, Callie sat cross-legged on the floor watching the special broadcast while the sacred white buffalo of Callie's bedtime story cavorted through Ricky's dreams.

And just outside, thanks to Mac Sanford, two security guards armed with riot guns stood sentinel to keep the unruly crowd at bay. After the broadcast they had descended on the barrio—thrill seekers, curiosity seekers, enraged citizens with baseball bats, intent on beating the truth out of the doctors who conspired to dupe the city.

"We interrupt your regular programming to bring you this special broadcast from the mayor's office in downtown Houston."

The camera panned across the four people assembled, Mayor Jim Dillard, Mac Sanford, Joseph and Peg. The mayor and Joseph looked dignified, the reporter, smug, while Peg looked like a high school cheerleader. Somebody you'd love to have an ice cream with after the game.

"Atta girl, Peg," Callie whispered.

Joseph had been right about using her on the broadcast.

Mac Sanford's face filled the screen as he began to talk.

"Pandemonium reigns in a city that just three hours ago learned the truth of what was happening in a Hispanic barrio on the east side of town. Traffic is backed up for two miles on Interstate 10 as people attempt to leave town. Police Chief Edward Rakestraw has doubled the number of cruise cars on the streets and tripled the number of patrolmen on the beat. But that's not enough. The citizens of this city are angry and scared. They want to know why they weren't told of the threat of a hot virus. They want answers.''

And you're the cause, Callie thought. But to give the reporter credit, he appeared sincere and concerned.

''And here to provide them,'' he said, ''is Mayor Jim Dillard and a team of virologists. Mayor, tell the people what's happening.''

Jim Dillard was smart. That much was obvious. He avoided using frightening terms such as *outbreak, hot virus, ebola, hemorrhagic fever.* Instead he calmly told of a rare virus, quickly diagnosed by the expert team led by Dr. Joseph Swift and quickly contained.

''There is no cause to panic. We have every reason to believe the crisis has passed,'' the mayor said. ''I urge you to remain calm.''

Mac turned his attention to Joseph. ''Dr. Swift flew in from Italy to combat this disease. Doctor, tell us more about this virus.''

Joseph, too, dodged around the scary aspects of the disease. Instead he focused on the symptoms, urged people to contact their doctors at the first signs. Then he deftly handed the ball to Peg.

''My associate, Peg Cummings, has witnessed remarkable recoveries. Peg…''

She smiled into the camera, and it panned close enough to show her dimples.

''First I want to say 'hi' to my husband in Atlanta.'' She waggled two fingers. ''Hi, Mike. Put the soup on, I'll be home soon.''

It was the perfect touch. After that inspired opening, she told about Ricky bouncing on his bed and demanding tacos.

Mac probed and prodded, but the team remained staunch in their positive presentation of a terrible situation.

"Doctor, should we all stay home and lock the doors?"

"No," Joseph said. "But for the next few weeks I would err on the side of caution. Don't go anywhere you don't have to. Avoid contact with others as much as possible."

"Doctor, is the virus airborne?"

Callie groaned. The reporter tapped into the fear of virologists worldwide—that no matter what they did to contain a hot virus, it would mutate and become airborne.

Joseph looked tired, and Callie's heart ached for him. It was bad enough that he spent twelve to fourteen hours a day at the hospital. Did he have to have this additional burden?

"No," he said. "The virus is not airborne."

"This concludes tonight's broadcast, but stay tuned for up-to-the-minute reports from Dr. Joseph Swift about the deadly virus that stalks our city."

Callie could have strangled Mac Sanford. Couldn't he have chosen less explosive words?

She waited up for her colleagues. Peg was exhausted and went straight to her trailer. Joseph looked as if he carried the entire world on his shoulders. Callie didn't say a word. Instead she opened her arms and he walked into her embrace.

They stood that way for a while, tightly wrapped together, her cheek against his chest, his cheek resting against her hair.

"Stay with me," he whispered.

Callie needed no explanation, no urging. He fell into bed fully clothed, and she lay beside him holding on, every muscle in her body, every inch of her skin communicating comfort and compassion.

Joseph woke with a start. The hands on the dial said 2:00 a.m. His clothes were constricting him, and it didn't take a genius to know the reason.

Callie.

She lay on her back, one arm across his chest and one leg flung across his hips. Her gown bunched around her hips and her legs looked silvery in the moonlight, the skin smooth and soft and fine.

His desire for her was painful. And painfully obvious.

Every bone, every muscle in his body ached for her. He longed to ease himself with her, to slide into that enticing body and give vent to every emotion he'd felt today—fear, outrage, despair, hope, lust, love.

While he'd battled through the mob outside the mayor's office and rode through the city under police escort, he had only one thought in mind—to be with Callie.

And when he'd walked into the trailer and she opened her arms, he knew: this woman held a piece of his heart. He would never be free of her, no matter how far he ran.

And yet, he couldn't take her. Not here. Not now.

Not ever.

Joseph clenched his jaw to hold back the groans. He willed himself to look away from her, away from the dewy skin, away from the midnight tumble of hair, away from her parted thighs and the enticing dark triangle.

The Bermuda Triangle.

If he ever entered, all would be lost. There would be no turning back. No denying. No recourse.

Callie. Callie.

He silently cried her name, and it echoed through the empty chambers of his heart. He could never have her, for that would mean risking loss so unthinkable he could never survive it. Not again.

Callie. Callie.

Joseph tightened his hold on her, buried his face in her hair and silently wept.

Chapter Nine

Joseph lay on his side, one arm pillowing his head, the other spread across the empty spot where Callie had been. One last look, she thought, one last touch. That's all she would allow herself.

Her fingers were gentle in his hair, her lips soft on his forehead.

She left him quickly, while he was still sleeping, for that was the only way Callie knew to handle a heart out of control.

Reality hit her the minute she stepped out of the trailer. Two guards immediately flanked her.

"Dr. Red Cloud? We're your escorts. Where do you want to go?"

"Only across the parking lot to the other trailer. Are you sure this is necessary?"

"Orders, ma'am."

There were no angry mobs in the early dawn, no wav-

ing baseball bats, no threatening posters. Nothing to indicate the crowds had ever been there except debris—
candy bar wrappers, empty chips bags, and soda bottles
tossed carelessly onto the sidewalk.

The sky lightened gradually from gray to a pink the
color of rose petals, and the sun topped the horizon to
shoot brilliant rays of gold across the parking lot. Mother
Nature forgiving her unruly children, spreading her beauty
over the ugliness of rage and disease.

Callie stopped in the middle of the parking lot to admire
the sky. She had always taken courage from nature, courage and hope. Perhaps it was her Apache upbringing, or
perhaps it was simply the way she was made.

Her father had taught the saying of Ohiyesa, a very wise
Santee Sioux: "All days are God's days, for only the
Great Spirit can make an arching rainbow or a roaring
waterfall or a bloodred sunset. Only the Great Spirit can
create the sublime."

Now, she stood silently with head uplifted. "It's beautiful, isn't it?"

"Ma'am?"

Callie shook her head, then continued toward the trailer.
Peg was already up and dressed.

"How did I do last night?" she asked.

"You were good, Peg. Very positive, very reassuring."

Peg laughed. "Just what the doctor ordered. Maybe
I've finally redeemed myself with Joseph."

"You redeemed yourself weeks ago—over there where
it really counts." Callie nodded in the direction of the
hospital.

"I'll be glad when it's all over. I miss Mike."

When it was over, Callie would never see Joseph again

except by chance. Perhaps in some other crisis, in some other city, in some other part of the world.

Perhaps never.

Suddenly she was envious of Peg and downright jealous. Why was it Peg could have everything and Callie nothing? Why did she have a wonderful man waiting at home for her, while Callie had nothing to look forward to except a lonely bed?

"Is something wrong, Callie? Is it something I said?"

"No. I'm tired, that's all."

"Aren't we all? It's my turn to see about breakfast. I'm going to drag myself over to the mess hall, pick up the phone and order take-out muffins and eggs."

"Sounds like a good plan to me."

After Peg left, Callie climbed into the shower and lifted her face to the sting of water. Cool water. She didn't want to be comfortable today. She needed to be shocked into a new day, alert and ready for battle on all fronts.

Joseph found Callie alone, which was exactly the way he wanted it. She had changed into jeans and a white shirt, and her hair was still wet from the shower. She looked radiant, and Joseph cursed the trickster fates.

"I didn't expect to see you again so soon." She glanced at her watch. "Not for another fifteen minutes anyway."

Something in his face gave him away, and her smile died. She put her hand on his arm.

"Joseph, what's wrong? Something's happened to Ricky."

"No. Not Ricky. It's your father, Callie. He's had a heart attack."

"Not Dad. Oh, God, not Dad!"

She crumpled, and he was selfishly glad to be the one there for her. He stroked her hair and soothed her with soft words.

Callie sobbed as if her heart were broken. He'd seen this happen many times, professionals who defied death every day, who could face an entire roomful of grieving relatives and deliver life-changing news with steadiness and calm, often folded when the situation applied to them.

Her weakness was only temporary, as he knew it would be.

"I have to go to him."

"Ron's sending a replacement for you, and I've already made your plane reservations."

"Do they know anything yet?"

"Not yet. The ambulance was there when your brother called."

She got her suitcase and began to throw her things inside.

"Is there anything I can do to help you?"

"You already have. Thank you, Joseph."

"You're welcome."

This was his cue to leave. He'd arranged for a limousine to take her to the airport. His job was finished here. His patients needed him.

But he couldn't leave. Not yet. Callie was going home and he might never see her again.

Three weeks ago that wouldn't have mattered. But one kiss had changed everything. Or was it before that? Had his life turned upside down and inside out the minute Callie Red Cloud stepped from the plane?

There was so much he wanted to say to her that he couldn't think where to begin. Callie saved him.

"This was never supposed to happen to my father."

"Disease respects no one."

"But his *heart*...Calder Red Cloud has the biggest, most generous heart in all the tribal lands. Ask anybody. They'll tell you."

"You love your father very much, don't you?" Joseph felt admiration tinged with a slash of envy.

"I love him more than I can describe. If he dies, part of me will die, too."

Joseph thought of a quiet hillside in Umbria, of wind stirring cypress and olive trees that watched over his late wife's grave. Part of him had died once, and he'd thought life would never be good again. Now Callie had him dreaming of possibilities, longing for home and hearth and children, hoping for a better future. And yet he knew such hopes and dreams were foolish.

He was crazy to think two people in their profession could have a normal relationship. There was too much risk, too much uncertainty.

Fate had brought her and fate was taking her away. Though he regretted the circumstances he knew it was best for both of them that she leave.

"Does Ricky know I'm leaving?"

"Yes."

"I'll stop by the trailer and say goodbye."

"Good."

"Tell Peg I'll call her."

"I will."

Until that moment he hadn't known that it was possible to die inside at the prospect of saying goodbye.

Her limousine slid into view.

"My car's here," she said.

"Yes." He was so full he could barely speak.

"I guess this is goodbye."

She stood before him, her face mirroring the agony he felt. If he touched her, if he kissed her, if he held her, he could never let her go.

"I guess it is. Goodbye, Callie. Take care."

"You, too."

He couldn't watch her leave. Instead he bolted out the back door of the trailer and strode toward the hospital. He had a hot virus to fight.

Thank God.

Ricky was sitting on Sister Beatrice's lap, coloring. When Callie walked in he pretended he didn't see her.

"Ricky..." He didn't look up. Callie knelt beside him and took his small hand. "I have to go now. My father is sick."

"Go on."

He kept his head ducked and his fist closed tightly around a black crayon. The picture he had been coloring was a spring scene with flowers and birds. He had colored everything black, including the sky.

"Ricky, look at me." Callie gently cupped his face and tipped it upward. "I love you very much."

"Tell me a story."

He was testing her. She plucked him off the Sister's lap and held him close.

"My car is waiting, and if I stay too long I'll miss my plane. Give me a goodbye hug, and I'll come back to see you as soon as I can."

"You promise?" Ricky stuck his lower lip out and balled his hands into fists. A little boy alone, ready to fight the world.

"I promise."

Callie didn't cry until she was in the limousine, then

she let the tears flow freely. In the quietness of the luxurious car she cried for Ricky, for her father, for Joseph and for herself.

By the time she reached the airport all her crying was done, and Callie Red Cloud boarded her flight home, head up and chin out.

Chapter Ten

Until she walked into the hospital in Tucson, Callie had never seen her father in a hospital bed. He looked shrunken, as if the illness had attacked more than his heart.

When he saw her, he smiled. "You didn't have to come. I saw the news last night. They need you in Houston."

"I'm here, Dad, where I belong."

"Humph." She saw right through him. The glisten in his eyes gave him away.

Callie wrapped him in a big hug, then turned to hold her mother close.

"How are you holding up, Mom?"

"Nothing like this has ever happened to Calder before." Ellen didn't try to disguise her tears. "I don't know what to do without your father."

"I'm right here, Ellen, and I don't plan on going anywhere for a very long time."

When Calder reached for his wife's hand, she quickly left her daughter to sit on the edge of her husband's bed.

That's the way it had always been with them, Callie thought. So much in love. Inseparable. Two hearts beating as one. When one heart failed, the other suffered.

Watching them she'd often felt like an intruder. But today, watching them she thought of Joseph. Why had fate put him in her path and then stacked the cards against them?

"Why don't you sit down, Sis? You look beat."

She sat down beside her brother, and he squeezed her hand. "Dad's a tough old bird."

"You two needn't talk about me as if I'm not even here."

Callie and Eric grinned at each other. Sickness might have made Calder's body look frail, but it had done nothing to his tart tongue and his sharp wit.

"What do the doctors say, Dad?" she asked.

"It's nothing but a posterior infarct," Calder told her. "I told you you shouldn't have come."

"They've checked the cardiac enzymes?"

"Once. Nurse Dracula will be here any minute to get her second gallon of blood."

"And?"

"Listen to her, Ellen. Like the Gestapo. Why did we ever encourage her to be a doctor?"

"Dad, you didn't answer my question."

"Enzymes are up."

Bewildered, Ellen turned to her daughter. "What does all this mean?"

Before she could answer, Calder reassured his wife. "It

means there's nothing wrong with me that diet and exercise can't cure.''

"Still…" Ellen paused.

Quickly she excused herself. "I think I'll go and get coffee. Anybody want a cup?''

"Make mine black and be sure you stir it with the feather of an eagle." Calder winked at his wife.

It was obvious that Ellen didn't know whether to laugh or cry.

"I'll be right back," she said.

"Take your time, Mom. Eric and I will watch after Dad.''

"Humph. I don't need watching after.''

"Doctors makes the worst patients," Callie told Eric.

"Especially Dr. Red Cloud.''

"I heard that. Damned right, I make a miserable patient. Lying here flat of my back when I ought to be out seeing about my own patients. That young whippersnapper I've got working in the clinic can't find his butt with both hands.''

"Now, Dad," Callie said. "He has excellent credentials. You told me so yourself.''

"Credentials don't mean much if you don't have any common sense.''

"It's not as bad as Dad says," Eric told his sister. "Dr. Brenner patches the twins up just fine.''

Eric's twin boys were hellions, five years old going on twenty-five, adventurous daredevils always breaking skin and bones tumbling from trees and rocks and bicycles and horses and anything else they could climb onto or get into.

"Humph." Calder wasn't about to give an inch.

Everything Eric said was true. His grandsons couldn't have better care if Calder himself did it, but he'd bite his tongue off before admitting it.

If complaining about Dr. Brenner could make Callie leave that dangerous job, he would complain until Mother Earth shed tears as big as basketballs.

Not that he wasn't proud of Callie. Far from it. Both he and Ellen were bursting with pride, and yet both of them desperately wanted their daughter to have all the things they had, a loving partner, children and time to enjoy family.

He knew what it was like to be totally dedicated to a job. He'd been that way himself once. His life had been well-ordered and productive, and he'd thought it was very good. Then he'd met Ellen.

It took only one encounter with that blue-eyed, blond-haired sprite to show him exactly what he was missing.

He'd fallen in love with her the minute he set eyes on her, and he loved her as much today as he had the day they met. Could any man be luckier?

"Eric, go down and be with your mother. She needs comforting."

Calder watched his tall, strong son. Blond, blue-eyed and a shade darker than fair of skin, he was more like his mother than Callie. She was Apache through and through. And stubborn to the bone. Just like Calder.

"Come here so I can look at you, Callie."

When she stood beside the window he saw the fatigue etched in her face.

"It's very bad down there, isn't it?"

"Yes."

Callie knew it would be useless to try to spare her father. He could always see through her, and he knew too much about medicine to be blind to the horrors of a hot virus.

"Those other virologists, Dr. Cummings and Dr. Swift. Are they good people to work with?"

"Yes. This is Peg's first field assignment, and she's sometimes a little shaky, but Dr. Swift is brilliant…and driven."

Something about the way his daughter said *Dr. Swift* made Calder sit up and take notice.

"He looks Native American. Is he?"

"Yes. Sioux. He's a full-blood."

Calder retreated into silence while he studied his daughter. She'd been in the field many times, and each time she returned home he saw the fatigue. But he saw something more today, pain and an odd sort of reserve that Callie wore like a cloak.

"Tell me what's going on down there," he said.

"The hospital is still full, but we think we've passed the crisis stage."

Calder shook his head. "I'm not talking about the hot virus. Tell me what's going on with you, Daughter."

When her father called her daughter, Callie knew he was searching for soul truths. He was not only her parent but her best friend and confidant. She had always told Calder everything.

But not now. He needed nothing on his mind except getting well.

She perched on the edge of his bed and took his hand.

"Dad, let's save all this until you get home, okay?"

"You're treating me like a sick old man. I despise that, Callie."

"No. I'm treating you like a patient who needs to concentrate on only one thing, making your body strong and healthy again."

As much as he hated to admit it, Calder was too tired to probe. Callie was smart. She would work things out, and when she was ready, she would come to him.

He opened his arms, and she put her head on his chest.

"I love you, Dad."

"I love you, Callie."

As he stroked her hair he made himself a promise: he would live to see his daughter happy, even if it meant giving up rib eyes and using that damnable treadmill Ellen kept in the corner of the bedroom.

Nurse Glenda Jernigan came into the room, all starch and efficiency.

"Good afternoon, Doctor." She picked up his wrist to check his pulse. "And how are we doing today?"

"I feel like Tarzan, ready to swing from vines and beat my chest, but you'll have to speak for yourself, Nurse Jernigan."

"Your father's a pistol."

"My hearing's good, too. Would you kindly include me in your remarks?"

Nurse Jernigan rolled her eyes. "Just for that I'm going to punch a few extra holes in you."

"You always do."

Callie was thrilled to see her father in such high spirits.

"Dad, behave yourself," she told him, laughing.

"Never. What kind of example would that be for a father to set for his children?"

That evening Callie and Eric convinced Ellen to go to the hotel and get some sleep while Callie stayed at the hospital with Calder.

"I don't need anybody here," he'd said, but Callie could tell he was pleased that she stayed.

He complained about the bed, he complained about the food, he complained about the view. That behavior was so unlike him that Callie finally called him to task.

"You're not a whiner, Dad, and there's nothing wrong with your bed or the food or the view, either, for that matter.'' Actually he had the best room in the hospital, a large sunny room with a view that overlooked the garden.

She sat on the edge of his bed and took his hand. ''So, what's the real problem?''

Calder looked sheepish. ''You'll think me a foolish old man.''

''I could never think that of you. You're my hero, always have been and always will be.''

''Someday you'll have another one.''

Joseph floated through Callie's mind, but she quickly shut him out.

''You're changing the subject. What's the problem, Dad?''

''Since Ellen and I married, we've never spent a night apart. I don't know if I can sleep without her.''

''I'll have the nurse give you something.''

''A pill's not the same as a wife.''

''There are some who would disagree.''

Calder chuckled. ''Not if they were married to Ellen. But I will have to say that some of your mother's relatives…''

The door banged open, and there stood Ellen, arms akimbo.

''What's this about my relatives?''

''Ellen! I thought you were at the hotel.''

''That's obvious.''

''When did you get back?''

''Don't you change the subject, Calder Red Cloud.''

She marched to his bed, and he snagged her hand. ''As I was saying, darling, some of your relatives are smart and pretty, but not a single one can hold a candle to you.''

Ellen giggled, then leaned down to kiss her husband. Watching them, Callie couldn't help but wonder about the choices she'd made in her own life.

"Mom, you shouldn't be here. I'm perfectly capable of taking care of Dad for one night."

"It's not a matter of capability, Callie. It's a matter of the right thing to do. I've never spent one single night away from your father and I don't intend to start now."

Ellen turned to Eric who was standing in the door, holding her night case.

"Eric, put my things in the closet. I'm not leaving this room again until Calder leaves."

Having had her say, Ellen settled in a chair beside Calder's bed and took her knitting out of her tote bag. Calder beamed.

"Sis, would you like a ride back to the hotel?"

"I might as well. It's obvious these two have everything they need."

Callie caught up with news of Eric's family over dinner. A journalist and editor of the tribal newspaper, Eric had a way with a story, and by the time dinner was over Callie was in stitches over the antics of the twins, Kevin and Clint.

"They're regular little savages," Eric said. "One of these days I expect to come home and find Brenda tied to a pole with a fire lit under her feet."

"How is she doing?" Brenda was a strong, quiet woman, as different from Callie as two women can be, but Callie liked her enormously.

"She's pregnant again, Callie."

Callie could picture how it would be with them, Eric plumping pillows behind Brenda's back and rubbing her swollen feet at night, fetching hot tea with cream and honey and drawing her bath in the early morning before the twins were stirring.

Eric was a kind and gentle man who loved deeply and wasn't afraid to show it.

Now he watched her expectantly, searching for some sign of joy or at the very least sisterly support, but all she could do was sit across from her brother and be miserable.

"Callie, what's wrong?"

"Nothing," she said, but Eric wasn't buying.

"Come on, Sis. I've pulled your chestnuts out of the fire too many times for you to start being evasive now."

"I don't want to talk about it."

"I think something's eating you up and you need to talk about it."

"Who appointed you my psychiatrist?"

"You did, when I was ten and you were five. Remember?"

"How could I forget?"

Callie started giggling. At five she'd been a spitfire, always getting into trouble at school. Unless the teachers sent a note home, Eric was the only one Callie told.

On that particular day, they'd made a blood pact to tell each other stuff and always be close.

"I'm thinking of adopting a little boy," she said.

"A baby?"

"No, he's four." At the memory of Ricky and Joseph, Callie wrapped her arms around herself…for warmth, for comfort, for reassurance, for reasons she couldn't even name.

"So many people died down there in Houston, Eric, but he survived."

One of things Callie loved most about her brother was the way he listened, with a waiting stillness that said in no uncertain terms, "I hear everything you say and I'm giving it my best thought."

She waited now, knowing that when he spoke his answer would carry the weight of his mind.

"I assume you're planning to do this as a single parent."

Callie hesitated only a moment. "Yes."

"Hmm."

"What does that mean?"

"I heard that hesitation. What does it mean?"

"Nothing. I've met someone, but it can never mean anything."

Eric pulled out his pipe and Callie watched his studied ritual, the careful tamping in of tobacco, the way he held match to the bowl just so, the slow ascent to his mouth.

"You'll make a wonderful mother, Callie."

"I don't know. Maybe I'm just fooling myself. Maybe I'm doing this for selfish reasons—my biological clock is ticking. I'm jealous of Brenda. I'm even jealous of Mom."

She pushed her hair from her face, watching for her brother's reaction.

"Surely you don't expect me to be shocked, Callie. After all these years?"

"Don't remind me of years, Eric."

He caught her hand. "I've told you what I think, and I mean that. I know you're going to give this a lot more thought, but please remember that I will support your decision one hundred percent. Whatever it is."

"Thanks, Eric."

He came around the table and kissed her cheek. "Gotta call home."

"Give Brenda my love."

In her room, Callie flipped on the television for company, then took a long hot shower. Afterward she fell across the bed, too tired to even put on her T-shirt.

Joseph had tried to find a moment to call Callie, but there hadn't been a minute in his hectic day. Between seeing to the needs of his patients and keeping an eye on the milling crowd outside, he'd had his hands full.

"I'll do it when I leave here," he muttered.

"Do what?" Peg asked.

"Call Callie...to check on her father."

"It's okay, Joseph. You're allowed to be human."

He could almost believe that was true. But the minute he stepped outside the hospital, he knew better.

The crowd surged forward, brandishing signs and screaming obscenities at him. A line of policemen tried to hold them back, but it was impossible.

A billy club whistled through the air. A knife answered it. Suddenly there was blood—and bedlam.

Joseph rushed forward to tend the wounded. A policeman nabbed his sleeve, yelling, "Get back!"

"I'm a doctor."

"I know who you are. You're the one they're after."

In times of tragedy that's the way it always was, Joseph thought. People had to have somebody to blame. He was the logical one. After all, hadn't they seen him on television? Hadn't he been named as the leader of the team of virologists?

Still, he'd taken the Hippocratic Oath. He jerked free and knelt beside a man with a gash on his head. If he hadn't been on his knees he might have seen what was coming.

Callie jarred awake. She'd fallen asleep without her clothes. As she reached for her gown, she froze, staring at the TV.

"Rioting broke out today in the east side of Houston where just yesterday Dr. Joseph Swift revealed a hot virus had struck."

The camera panned the angry mob. In the background was the hospital, and just coming out the door was Joseph.

"Liar!" someone yelled at him. Then, "Murderer!"

"Oh, God," Callie said.

Pandemonium broke loose in Houston. Callie jumped off the bed and knelt in front of the TV set trying to find Joseph in the crowd. It didn't take long.

His image filled the screen, his face anguished. Callie had seen that look so many times. A man was down, hurt, and two policeman couldn't restrain Joseph. He was a doctor and he was bound to do his duty.

Callie touched the TV screen and traced the lines of his beloved face.

Beloved. It came as a shock to her how easily she thought of him in that way. She tested the word aloud, and while the word was on her lips, everything exploded.

Simultaneously a gunshot sounded and the crowd erupted. Blood bloomed on the front of a policeman's shirt as another shot rang out.

"Joseph! Where's Joseph?"

In a panic Callie watched the crowd push and shove their way toward freedom. Another shot sang out, and above it all a calm voice-over:

"Six people were injured at the riot, two policeman and Dr. Joseph Swift."

Callie moaned. "Not Joseph. Please God, not Joseph."

"Patrolman John Lindley was treated and released from Houston General while Patrolman Marvin Hanshaw remains in critical condition."

"What about Joseph?" Callie whispered. All the blood left her face, and she felt faint.

As if in answer to her question, the camera panned in for a close-up of Joseph being carried off on a stretcher.

"If he's gone I will die," Callie said.

"Dr. Joseph Swift sustained a head wound...."

Tears poured down Callie's face, and it wasn't until the newscast was over that she could find strength to get off the floor.

She stumbled to the phone and had to dial three times before she got the number right.

"Hello," she said, but she could do nothing more than stand in the middle of the room and shiver with relief.

"Hello? Is anyone there?"

"Oh, God, Joseph, I thought you were dead."

"Callie?"

"I saw the riot on television."

"I was on my way to call you. How's your father?"

It's you I want to talk about, she wanted to scream, and in that split second Callie knew that what her father had told was true: she would find another hero.

"He's complaining, and that's a good sign. All tests indicate a posterior infarct."

"That's good."

Callie's hand tightened on the receiver. "What about you?"

"I have a nasty scratch, that's all. And I have a helluva headache," he said with a chuckle.

"You're laughing."

"Not at you, Callie."

"But you're *laughing*."

Callie wanted to hit him, she wanted to punch his lights out, she wanted to stomp on his toes. Hard.

"Posttraumatic hysteria," Joseph said.

"It's not funny."

"No, it's not. I'm so damned glad you were not here, Callie. God, if anything happened to you..."

Silence. She gripped the phone, breathless.

What, Joseph? What? her mind screamed, but she said nothing.

He finally cleared his throat, and she eased her death grip on the phone.

"How's Ricky?" she asked.

"He's fine, though a little sulky since you've been gone."

"Does he ask about me?"

Joseph laughed. "Approximately every five minutes. Mainly he wants to know when you're coming home."

Home. A place where loved reigned. A safe spot where you could shut out the rest of the world simply by closing the door and walking into the arms of your beloved.

How easily she'd been fooled into believing the house trailer the three of them shared in Houston, Texas was home.

There was another long silence, and she wondered if Joseph was thinking the same thing.

"I promised him I would be back," she said. "Tell him that, Joseph. I *will* be back."

"I'll call you tomorrow...to check on your dad."

"Joseph..." Visions of riots and danger and death swirled in her head. "What's being done to prevent another uprising?"

"Callie, don't worry about us. This whole area's so tightly sealed that a rat would have a hard time getting inside."

"All right, Joseph I won't worry. Take care."

"You, too, Callie."

It was only after she hung up that Callie realized she hadn't inquired about Peg. What was wrong with her?

She knew, of course. It was a thing called love. It narrowed your focus so that no matter where you turned, no matter where you looked, all you could see was one person.

Your beloved.

Chapter Eleven

Brenda and the twins came over for Calder's homecoming. She'd made pasta, salad and fruit turnovers. "All low fat," she said. And the twins had made an enormous banner that hung from the front porch: Welcome Home, Big Daddy.

"What's all this?" Calder stood in the middle of his driveway admiring his mountain, his house, his family, his sign. Life was good, he decided, and it was going to get even better. Today Eric had told him about Brenda's pregnancy.

The twins wrapped themselves around his legs, and Brenda walked into his embrace.

"What a homecoming. I guess I'll have to get sick more often."

"Don't you dare," Ellen said.

There was a general happy hubbub while Eric stowed

away the luggage. Calder endured it with all the patience he could muster then he got down to business.

He grabbed his coat and his hat off the rack by the door and kissed Ellen on the cheek.

"I'll be back in a little while," he said.

"Where do you think you're going?"

"I'm going down to the clinic to see if Dr. Brenner has killed all of my patients."

"Dad," Callie chided. "He's not that bad."

"Come and see for yourself."

It tickled him that Callie didn't hesitate. If he played his cards right he might woo her back home.

And then to his clinic.

The tribal lands could use another good doctor. A Red Cloud had been their medicine man since the Apaches settled in the mountains.

Callie took his arm, and on the way down the curving path, Calder leaned a little heavier on her arm than he needed to. He liked to see a good tradition carried on, and he wasn't above a little blackmail to do it.

The clinic stood in the midst of towering pine and birch trees with a stream meandering so close to the front door you had to walk over a small bridge to enter the foyer. As Callie stepped inside she was immediately transported back to her youth, back to days of standing at her father's side while he explained the difference between simple and multiple fractures, of playing hide-and-seek with Eric in the medicine closet, of memorizing the names of medicines as if it were a game, of knowing the names and the life histories of all the patients who came through the doors of Big Bend Clinic.

Now she knew very few of the names and none of the histories. She'd been gone too long.

"Welcome back, Dr. Red Cloud."

The man who greeted them was Doug Brenner, Calder's assistant. He was young, earnest, frazzled and nothing at all like her father had said. Within five minutes Callie knew he was a jewel, and as soon as they got back home she told her father so.

"You should be ashamed of yourself, Dad, denigrating a fine young doctor like that."

"Maybe I did exaggerate a little. I'm sorry, Daughter."

"You don't look one bit remorseful. In fact, you look rather pleased with yourself."

Ellen stepped in, of course. She always did when Calder was under attack.

"Your father's just glad to be home, Callie. And if you two are going to talk nothing but medicine I'll have to intervene. He needs to relax."

"You're right, Mom. I'm sorry."

Chapter Twelve

The last of the dead were buried, and the survivors had
returned to their homes. In the trailer across the lot Peg
Cummings was packing her bag for home. Callie's replacement, Glen Sullivan, had left early that morning.

Now came the hardest part of Joseph's job. Saying
goodbye to Ricky. Without any surviving relatives he was
now a ward of the State of Texas, soon to be consigned
to the care of the Department of Human Services.

It all sounded so cold, so impersonal. And yet the
woman assigned to Ricky's case was neither. Jenine Rayborn was younger than Joseph had expected, early forties
he guessed, and she exuded a warmth that put him at ease.

"Don't you worry about a thing, Dr. Swift. We'll take
good care of your little boy."

"He's special and still fragile."

"I can assure you that we have the best medical care
available to our wards twenty-four hours a day."

Ward. Joseph inwardly cringed. He despised hearing Ricky described that way.

"Very few survive the virus he had." The woman nodded as if to say she understood. Still, Joseph was not satisfied. He pulled out a business card, scrawled his home number in Italy, his mother's number in South Dakota, his beeper number.

"Call me if anything unusual develops with him, anything at all."

"I'll try, but I can't make any promises."

That was the thing. Once Joseph handed Ricky over to the state, he also relinquished control. Whatever happened to Ricky was totally out of his hands.

Jenine glanced at her watch, a clear indication the interview was over.

"I'll come by to pick up the boy this afternoon, Doctor."

Joseph didn't want it to be this way: Ricky riding off to a strange place with a strange woman.

"No," he said.

Jenine's expression tightened, and Joseph berated himself for sounding harsh and dictatorial. If he ever had any skills of diplomacy, now was the time to use them.

"Forgive me, Miss Rayborn, I didn't mean to snap at you. It's been a rough ride."

He didn't have to feign fatigue in order to gain sympathy. Jenine's smile stretched wide.

"I understand. No offense taken."

"I'd like to make this transition as painless as possible. Ricky has had a difficult time."

"Most of our wards do, Doctor."

"If you don't mind, I'd like to bring Ricky here, walk through his room with him, help him feel less abandoned."

"Regulations…" Jenine paused, studying him. "I guess this once won't hurt. What time can I expect you?"

"Four o'clock."

"Fine. I'll see you then."

Joseph was sweating when he left her office, and he blamed it on the Texas heat. He glanced at his watch. Twelve o'clock. That left him four hours to spend with Ricky, four hours to convince the child that everything was going to work out all right.

He wished he could convince himself.

"I'm not going."

Ricky stood with his back to the wall, hands balled into fists and back bowed up for a fight as he made his sentiments known in no uncertain terms.

In order to get down to the child's level, Joseph was kneeling. He'd been on his knees for the last two hours and he was beginning to get stiff. He hated being stiff.

As a matter of fact, he hated being forty, he hated his job and he hated the State of Texas. Right now all he wanted was to be in his bed at home with the casement windows wide open and nothing in his view except a grove of olive trees and sunflowers as far as the eye could see.

"Ricky, Miss Rayborn is a very nice woman, and she'll take good care of you."

"Why do I have to go with her?"

"We've been through all that, Ricky."

"I want to go with you."

"I live in Italy. There are laws that say I can't take you out of the country."

"We'll run fast and they won't catch us."

"Italy is across the ocean. I'll be flying home."

"I'll hide in your suitcase."

Sighing, Joseph glanced at his watch. Another hour, and he had to be in Jenine Rayborn's office with Ricky.

There was nothing else to do except admit that his plan was a total failure. And that was something he hadn't had to do in a long while.

"I wish it could be different, Ricky."

Something in his attitude must have tipped Ricky, for he collapsed against Joseph, sobbing.

"I want you to be my daddy. I want Callie. Where's Callie?"

"Her father got sick, and she had to go home."

"She promised she'd come back. She promised."

"Not all promises can be kept, Ricky."

It was called being an adult, and it was one of the saddest rites of passage in a person's life—the moment he realized that fate had a way of negating even the most heartfelt promises.

I will keep you safe always, he'd told Maria. *I promise.*

"I want Callie," Ricky sobbed.

Joseph held the little boy next to his heart, and in that moment he knew that's where the child would always be. They had forged a bond that couldn't be broken by time or distance or the laws of the U.S. government.

"I want Callie, too, pal, but we don't always get what we want. That's another sad fact of life."

The air conditioner worked overtime in the trailer, muting sound so that street traffic was nothing more than a hum, like the persistent drone of mosquitoes. Closer by, there was the sound of a car door slamming. Then suddenly she was there—Callie, standing in the doorway with a teddy bear in one hand and her suitcase in the other.

Stunned, Joseph sat on his haunches staring. Ricky didn't suffer the same paralysis. He launched himself at Callie with squeals of joy.

"I knew you'd come back," he said.

Callie squatted beside the small boy to hug him, but over the top of her head she watched Joseph. Why didn't he say something? Why didn't he do something?

"Of course I came back, Ricky. I'll always come back to you."

Did Joseph know she was talking about him, too? His eyes were dark and watchful, and he had the waiting sort of stillness she'd seen in panthers stalking prey in the mountains.

Moving with the lithe grace of one of the big cats, Joseph stood up.

"Welcome home, Callie," Joseph said.

To anyone else, it might have seemed a strange choice of words, calling this godforsaken place home, but Callie fully understood his meaning. The three of them had made a crude trailer in a parking lot a haven.

"Miss me?" she said.

Her racing heart belied her teasing tone, and Joseph waited for a long time before answering. Heat flushed her face and neck.

"More than you'll ever know."

There was nothing lighthearted about his answer. Just the opposite. His eyes, his face, his whole body spoke of hunger so great it left her breathless.

She longed for one moment alone with him. One touch. One caress. One kiss.

Just one.

But Ricky had pressing things on his mind, things that demanded immediate attention.

"Callie, can I go home with you?"

The distraction was a welcome relief. Longing for things she knew she couldn't have was destructive. Yearning for the forbidden would only bring her pain.

"What's this all about?" she said, and Joseph told her.

She'd arrived in Houston just in time to say goodbye again, this time to Ricky. Should she tell him of her decision? Should she say, I want you to be mine?

She quickly decided, no. A morass of legal red tape had to be untangled before she could adopt Ricky, and who knew what would happen along the way? Best not to make a promise to a child that she might not be able to keep.

Ricky withdrew into sullen silence during Joseph's explanation, and he remained steadfastly there, even when both of them bent over to reassure and comfort him.

"I'll come to see you as often as I can," Joseph said.

Tears glistened on Ricky's cheeks. Callie wiped them away with the tips of her fingers.

"You know we will always love you, Ricky. And I'll come see you, too, as much as possible."

Ricky turned his face away from them. Pain ripped at Callie, and she sought to ease her own by easing his.

"I'm sure Miss Rayborn will find the you the best mommy and daddy possible," she said.

"Why can't I have you?"

Ricky's question haunted Callie all the way downtown. Here was a child who had lost everything he loved. Nothing left to him was familiar except the two people in the car.

He rode beside them stoic. Once he'd realized it was useless to fight, he retreated behind a wall of silence.

Joseph was equally silent, his hands tight on the wheel, his jaw clenched. Callie smoothed Ricky's hair, touched his cheek, patted his knee, squeezed his hand. Anything to reassure him.

And herself.

Callie had no intention of telling Joseph her plans. The

last thing she wanted was for Joseph to think she was using Ricky as a means to get to him.

No, Joseph would fly back to Italy and she would pursue her plans alone, just as she always had.

She'd known from the beginning how it would end. What she hadn't counted on was the pain. How could a heart hurt so much and still go on beating?

Joseph wanted the separation to come quickly.

Jenine Rayborn was waiting for them. She'd obviously had experience with tangled goodbyes, for she quickly took over with Ricky. Joseph barely had time for one last hug.

"Goodbye, pal. See you soon."

"Bye, Joe."

Such a forlorn little face. Joseph walked away quickly. Now there was nothing standing between him and freedom except Callie.

In spite of his intentions, when the time came he couldn't bear to say a quick goodbye in the sterile atmosphere of the Texas Department of Human Services.

"I'll go with you to the airport," she said.

"Fine."

Silently he cursed himself for sounding curt, but that was better than the alternative, that was better than showing his true feelings.

Mercifully the ride to the airport was short. Outside the cab he grabbed his bag and hung on as it were a life raft.

"Well, Callie, this is it," he said.

He knew he sounded like something out of a grade B movie, but he was too numb to care. He envied Callie's self-possession. Was it because she didn't care? Because she cared too much?

Joseph would never know. He would never ask.

"Yes," she said. "This is goodbye—again."

If it hadn't been for the sun he might have lifted one hand in sardonic salute, then walked away. But the sun chose exactly that moment to angle itself westward and become a sunset so brilliant, so blindingly beautiful it looked as if it had been painted by an artist.

And Callie was right in the center. A thing of awesome, aching beauty. How could he leave her without touching her?

"Callie…" His suitcase slid to the ground, and she stood before him, breathless. "I don't want to leave like this…so abruptly."

"I don't want you to…"

To stay? To go? To kiss me? What was she going to say, and why did she stop herself?

"I hate goodbyes," he said. Especially to you, Callie.

He could never say what he was thinking to Callie. Never. He had no right.

"So do I," she said.

Time crystalized. Caught in that diamond-bright web he saw not merely the moment but every moment he had spent with her—the embrace under the cocoon of blankets, the hands linked across the space between their narrow beds, the kiss.

To kiss her again. That's what he wanted. To kiss her and never let go.

And yet…

"You'll miss your plane," she said.

"Yes. Don't want to do that. It's a long way home."

A very long way. Especially without Callie.

"Goodbye, Joseph."

Her face was tilted upward. It would be so easy to kiss her, so easy.

And so hard to let go.

He touched her cheek, softly, trailed his fingertips downward, across her lips. She parted them slightly, tasting him, and he died a little inside.

"Goodbye, Callie."

He left quickly, while he still could, left her standing in the sunset with her lips slightly parted, left without looking back.

He could never look back. He knew that. Only forward to the next outbreak, the next hot virus, the next battle, on and on until he was exhausted in mind and body. And someday, if was very lucky, he might forget about a bewitching woman named Callie Red Cloud.

Chapter Thirteen

Callie's file was open on Jenine Rayborn's desk. Jenine picked up the application and studied it as if she were looking for some clue she might have missed the first time around.

"Dr. Red Cloud," she said.

So formal, Callie thought. That wasn't a good sign. Or was it? Callie tried not to look as nervous as she felt.

"You have very impressive credentials."

"Thank you, Miss Rayborn."

Jenine closed the folder and studied Callie over the tops of her reading glasses. "If I were ever misfortunate enough to come in contact with one of these rare viruses, I'd certainly want you as my doctor."

"Thank you."

Why were they discussing her medical prowess? Didn't Jenine Rayborn want to know what kind of home she planned to give Ricky? What kind of parenting skills she had? What kind of education she could provide, what kind of advantages?

"Your work is very dangerous, isn't it, Dr. Red Cloud?"

"Certainly there are risks, but isn't living itself a risk?"

Jenine smiled. "Well said. But then, I expected no less from you." She took off her glasses, then went to the coffeemaker. "Coffee?"

"No, thank you. I don't drink it."

"My goodness. How do you manage to keep going?"

"Diet, exercise, overall good health. I keep myself in optimum condition, Miss Rayborn. I work hard, but I know how to make the most of my leisure time. I can provide a very good home for Ricky."

"I have no doubt about that. You could give him everything money can buy."

Callie resented that remark, but she was careful not to let her feelings show. A little boy's future hung in the balance.

"I can give him more than that, Miss Rayborn. I can give him love. I can be a real mother to him, and isn't that the most important thing here? Finding a home where Ricky will be loved?"

Jenine sat behind her desk and sipped her coffee.

"Not entirely. I've seen the two of you together. It's obvious you love him, Dr. Red Cloud."

Jenine set her cup in the saucer and focused her full attention on Callie. "What is also obvious to me is that you will not be a full-time parent, not with your kind of work."

Callie had expected this argument, and she was fully prepared to make a case for herself, and for Ricky.

"Many homes have two parents in demanding professions such as medicine and law," she said, "but they also have the resources to provide the very best care while they are away. Statistics show that quality is more important in terms of time spent with a child than quantity.''

Jenine's face gave nothing away. Callie decided she must have been a card shark in another life.

''Everything you say is true, of course, but as you said, you are talking about two-parent families.'' Jenine sipped her coffee, made a face, then poured a fresh cup. ''I can't abide cold coffee.

She slid behind her desk once more. ''Now, as I was saying, Dr. Red Cloud, you're making an application as a single parent. Is that correct?''

''Yes, that's correct.''

''There will be no father for Ricky?''

Callie had a vision of Joseph playing the guitar while Ricky sat in his lap, but she quickly shut her mind to what might have been.

''No, there will be no father. But I have a very close, very loving family. My own father is living, as is my mother. My brother and his wife and two boys live next door. I can assure you, Miss Rayborn, that Ricky will have the love and support of family at all times.''

''Doctor, what I have to look at is the parent adopting the child, and in your case, the parent seeking adoption will not be available to the child much of the time.''

Callie had heard all this before, but not from Ms. Rayborn. From her own mother: ''Callie, you don't have time to spend with your family. I know you love your work, but I hate to see it consume you.''

Callie had never considered doing anything else—until now. Until she was faced with the prospect of losing Ricky.

She hesitated only a moment before responding to Jenine's argument.

"What if I told you that I am considering leaving the field of virology and taking up practice with my father in a small clinic in Apache Tribal Lands?"

Could she really do it? Reason balked but the heart said *yes*.

"I can only go by the facts. You are a virologist, you are in the field much of the time and you are at high risk." Jenine shook her head. "I'm sorry, Dr. Red Cloud."

Defeat was galling to Callie, but this was more than merely not winning. This was a loss with such sweeping consequences that she didn't even want to think about them right now.

"Can I continue to see him?"

"Yes. As long as he is a ward of the state. Afterward...well, that would be up to the family who adopts him."

Callie escaped to the bathroom to collect herself before her visit with Ricky. He would surely ask to go home with her.

How do you tell a little child that the rules of a bureaucracy take precedence over the tenets of love?

Callie thought immersing herself in work would ease the pain, but she was wrong. There was a deep dark void inside her, and nothing she did could fill it.

Some days the emptiness was so bad she found herself actually wishing for another outbreak so she wouldn't have time to think about anything except fighting a hot virus...and possibly teaming up again with Joseph.

"Time for a break," Peg said, interrupting her thought.

Callie headed to the refrigerator for a cup of orange juice and Peg headed straight to the point.

"Pour me one, too, then sit over here and talk." She patted the sofa. "You've been miserable ever since we got back from Houston and I want to know why. And don't you tell me it's just fatigue or worry over your father, because I know better.''

''If you know all the answers why did you ask the question?''

''Because I want to hear you admit that you're human like the rest of us.''

''What does that mean?''

''I saw how it was with you and Joseph in Texas, and what's this all about, you flying off to Houston every weekend?''

''Ricky misses me, and I miss him.''

''Every weekend? Come on, Callie. I like Ricky, too, but don't you think that's excessive? Besides, you know the rules. Don't get emotionally involved with patients.''

''Ricky's more than a patient to me.''

''I see.'' Peg was thoughtful for a moment. ''And what about Joseph? Was he more than a colleague?''

''No.''

Peg snorted, and Callie jumped off the sofa.

''All right. All right. He was. What does any of this matter? He's in Italy and I'm in Atlanta, and as far as I'm concerned it's over.''

''Is it?''

''Yes,'' Callie said, but she shook her head no.

''Well, I guess that's definitive.'' Peg rinsed their glasses then put them in the dishwasher. ''Mike's grilling steaks this weekend. Want to come?''

''Sorry. I can't.''

''Don't tell me. You're flying back to Houston.''

Since coming back to Atlanta, Callie had retreated into a safe cocoon of silence. It was the only way she could handle her pain: pretend nothing had happened in Houston, pretend she had returned to work as she always did, her spirit high and her heart intact.

Peg caught Callie's hand. "You want to know something, Callie?"

"What?"

"When I first came to work at the center I thought you were some kind of deity. You're so smart, so self-assured, so focused. I was in awe of you. Still am, sometimes."

She squeezed Callie's hand. "Don't shut me out, Callie. Let me be the kind of friend to you that you've been to me. Everybody needs somebody."

Sometimes, Callie thought, a truth will hit you with such force you wonder why you never thought of it before.

"Thanks, Peg," she said.

"For what? I didn't do anything yet."

Everybody needs somebody.

"Yes, you did. I was going to Houston this weekend. I still am. But after that, I'm going home. I need some time to think about a lot of things."

"Good girl. I'm sure Ron will approve. He's been worried about you, too." Peg cocked her head to study Callie. "Will you be back?"

Would she? Callie told her friend the truth.

"I don't know."

Chapter Fourteen

The only reason he was flying back to America was to see Ricky. That's what Joseph kept telling himself.

"Liar," his mind whispered. Callie had been with him every waking moment since he left Texas. Her face in every sunflower, her laughter in every breeze, her tears in every dewdrop. Nothing he did could obliterate her, and that astonished Joseph.

Italy belonged to Maria. It was her homeland, the place where they had loved and lived, the place where she was buried.

He'd visited her windswept grave the day before he left. The stone angel that kept watch had grown mossy, but the rosebush he'd planted was in full bloom.

As he knelt in the soft earth he'd expected the old pain, the old guilt, the old rage. Instead he felt a lurching inside himself, a lifting, a letting go.

"Goodbye, Maria," he whispered.

A white dove flew down from the ancient tiled roof of the nearby church, then perched in the rosebush and murmured to him with soft throaty sounds. Though the air had been perfectly still moments earlier, a breeze brushed against his cheek and whispered in his ear.

Maria was giving her blessing.

Joseph had smiled, and he was smiling still when his plane landed in Houston.

The second thing he noticed, the thing that ripped his heart, was the forlorn quality of the little boy. Ricky had always been an exuberant child, even after he was orphaned.

"Ricky." The little boy looked up. "Surprise."

Joseph expected a quick rush across the room, then a bear hug. Instead Ricky flashed a big grin that quickly faded.

"Hi, Joe."

"Is that all I get?" Joseph sat on the edge of the bed and draped his arm around the thin shoulders. "Just a plain old hi."

Ricky cocked his head, studying Joseph solemnly. "You want to see my bear? Callie gave it go me."

He pulled a bedraggled and well-loved plush teddy bear from underneath his pillow. "See. I call him Homer."

"That's a good name."

"Homer can run fast." Ricky raced around the room with his teddy bear to demonstrate, then hopped back onto the bed.

"He can really run. Maybe he'll grow up to be a long-distance sprinter."

"I got a splinter once. Callie took it out." Ricky cocked his head to study Joseph. "She comes to see me every

Saturday.'' Every cell in Joseph's body went on alert.
"Why don't you come every Saturday?''

"It's a long way to Italy. Even on the plane.''

"Callie flies from Atlanta. She told me.'' Ricky stuck
out his chin, not giving an inch. "She loves me.''

"I love you, too, pal.''

"The Smiths don't love me.''

Joseph listened as if Jenine Rayborn hadn't already told
him about her first attempt to find parents for Ricky.

"I'm sure they love you, it just takes some people
longer to show it, that's all.''

"No, they don't 'cause I poured ink on Miz Smith's
white rug. She screamed and Miss Rayborn took me
away.''

Ricky made his announcement without sentiment, but
Joseph read between the lines—a little boy, feeling abandoned and unloved, defying the rules that made him a
ward of the state any way he knew how.

Reluctant to leave this child of his heart, he stayed until
bedtime, and by then Ricky's naturally sunny nature had
returned. In spades. He demanded good-night kisses and
hugs and three bedtimes stories.

When he left, Ricky was drifting asleep. Joseph hurried
toward the office and found Jenine Rayborn still there.
For once the fates were smiling on him.

"Did you have a good visit?'' she asked.

"Yes. He told me Callie always visits on Saturday.''

All the unspoken questions were in his face. Where is
she? What time does she come? Will I see her if I wait?

"Every Saturday, like clockwork. Except that awful
weekend he was with the Smiths, of course.''

Joseph stood in the doorway, waiting, waiting.

"Oh…she's already been here.'' Jenine checked her
records. "This morning, as a matter of fact. She didn't

stay as long today, said she had to catch a plane to Tucson.''

Callie had just finished her dinner of fish caught straight from the stream beside her tent and a potato baked on the coals of her fire. Yawning she leaned back against a cypress tree and stretched her moccasined feet toward the warmth of the blaze. It was chilly in the mountains at night.

In the distance an owl hooted, and from the underbrush nearby came the scurrying sounds of small night creatures hurrying about their business. Overhead the stars were brilliant in a sky as deep and dark as velvet.

Peace. That was exactly what she needed. Peace and a time to heal.

The mountains did that to a person. Was it only yesterday she'd made her camp up here? It seemed like weeks. Serious thinking would come later, she knew, but for now she was letting herself flow with the universe, letting go, letting herself embrace each moment and enjoy it to the fullest.

Callie closed her eyes, listening to the murmur of the brook and the soft soughing of the wind in the trees. Suddenly the tranquility was shattered by an eruption of sound—hooves thundering, branches snapping, earth shaking.

''What on earth?'' Callie jumped up just as one of her father's stallion's came crashing into the campsite.

''Thunderbolt! What are you doing here?''

The stallion tossed his head and whinnied. Callie eased in close and took his bridle. Her dad had never lost his seat on a horse, and yet why else would Thunderbolt be at her camp? Ellen would never attempt to ride him, preferring instead her staid and steady mare. Eric had his own mount.

Callie rubbed his muzzle. "What's up boy? What's wrong with you?"

"You're giving comfort to the wrong animal."

At the sound of that familiar voice, Callie whirled around, and there was Joseph, disheveled and panting. Her heart took wings, and she dared reason to clip them.

"You were the one on this horse?"

"Don't you dare laugh, Callie Red Cloud."

How could she help it? She'd thought she might never see Joseph again, and yet there he was, standing in the middle of the White Mountains, six feet away from her campfire.

There were a dozen questions she wanted to ask him— why he was here, how did he find her, what were his plans—but that would come later. He was here, and that was all that mattered.

"I've never heard of an Indian who can't keep his seat on a horse," she said.

"That animal is not a horse, he's a demon. I think your father lent him to me on purpose."

Joseph's hair had grown longer since she'd seen him. She liked him that way. It made him look even sexier than he had in Texas, and every inch Sioux.

He was still standing across the clearing, and in the blaze from the campfire he looked like some rugged and glorious god, hell-bent on a dangerous quest.

Callie flicked her tongue over lips suddenly gone dry.

"And what would that purpose be?"

The look Joseph gave her sent shivers down her spine.

"To keep me from doing what I'm planning on doing with his daughter."

His black eyes challenged, but Callie wasn't about to back down.

"And what is that?" she said.

"Make beautiful music."

Every atom in her body cried out for him. Her hands tightened on the stallion's reins.

"Then I hope you brought your guitar."

Joseph's smile was slow and easy, predatory in a way she'd never seen.

Perhaps it was the setting, perhaps it was the mood, perhaps it was lust, pure and simple. Whatever the reason, Callie accepted the inevitable. No, welcomed it.

"I don't need a guitar for the kind of music I have in mind," he said.

Joseph stalked her, and what she saw in his eyes was pure magic.

"You won't be needing these." Joseph pried the reins from her tight fingers, then raked her into his arms. Her breath shooshed out as he flattened her against his chest.

He planted his mouth down on hers in a way that brooked no argument.

Who wanted to argue? Callie was a starving woman suddenly turned loose in a banquet hall. He kissed her deeply, urgently, and she responded in kind. His lips devoured, his tongue probed. Holding on as if he would never let go, he kissed her until they both lost their breath.

Then they leaned back and stared at each other, too stunned for words. With a sound more animal than human, he took her again, his mouth punishing, bruising in the intensity of his hunger.

She swayed against him, a young sapling bending with the wind. Every muscle in his body was rigid. Pressed so tightly against him she could hardly breathe, she felt every sinew, every bone, every sharp angle.

With his mouth locked on hers he tangled his fingers in her hair, holding her captive while he played his heart-breaking brand of magic.

Somewhere in the distant regions of Callie's mind she heard echoes of the old questions. Why did Joseph deny his heritage? Why was he breaking his vow of not involving himself with another virologist? Did the old rules still hold?

But she was too far gone to ask the questions. Perhaps she never would ask them.

She needed what Joseph was giving, wanted what he offered. No questions. No promises. No holds barred.

His hips took up the urgent rhythm of his tongue, and Callie strained against him, trying to feel him, all of him, through their layers of clothes.

As if he had read her mind, Joseph ripped aside her shirt, scattering buttons to the four winds. She was braless and his eyes blazed as he lowered his lips to her breast. Callie arched her back, a bold honey-colored goddess offering herself to him. His lips closed over her, and he took her nipple deep in his mouth.

It was not enough. For either of them.

They ripped aside their clothes and with one accord fell to the ground. Wild in their need, the only sounds they made were akin to those of a mating stallion covering his mare.

Joseph's first thrust drove her back into the ground, and she arched high to meet him. Beads of sweat gathered on his face and dripped into the valley between her breasts. Callie dug her fingernails into his back and hooked her legs over his shoulders.

Her cries echoed through the darkened mountains, and Joseph held her on the burning edge until she was trembling. Then it started all over again, the rhythm escalating until her blood was singing once more.

Rolling over, he took her with him. She needed no words, no commands. She rode as if she owned the world, as if everything she knew and loved was held tightly inside.

Golden, glorious, glowing. That's how she felt.

The stars were no longer in the sky. They had fallen one by one and lodged in her heart. And there they would remain.

Forever.

She said none of this aloud, for instinct told Callie that Joseph had not come to talk about forever. Instead, she kept the secrets in her heart while she kept the flame in her body.

Joseph moaned and writhed beneath her, then lacing his fingers through hers, he squeezed. Hard.

"Now, Callie. Now!"

They erupted at the same time. The explosion shook Callie to her very marrow. Limp and sated, her legs trembling, her heart pounding, she fell against him and rested her cheek on his chest.

Wrapping his arms tightly around her, he pushed her damp hair back from her hot face. Neither of them spoke. The wind picked up speed, branches whispered, and Joseph's stallion whinnied.

"We must tether him," she said.

"Later." Joseph's arms tightened. "If I ever let you go I'm afraid I might lose you."

"Don't let go," Callie whispered. "Don't let go."

Joseph was in heaven. He was in hell.

After once having this woman, how could he ever let her go? And yet, he knew he must.

Need had driven him to her mountain. Need and a passion so great it bordered on obsession.

But nothing had changed for them. Not her job, not his. Their clash over heritage was there, simmering just beneath the surface. The old fears still lingered. The old problems remained.

For the moment, though, she was his. Her skin melted into his, her breath mingled with his, her heart beat a perfect rhythm with his. There in the mountains with the moon and stars as their witnesses they were united in heart and body as surely as if they had taken sacred vows. Nothing could change that, and nothing could take it away.

A chill wind blew across them, and Callie shivered. Without a word, Joseph carried her inside the tent and laid her upon a blanket the colors of the earth. It was handwoven with Apache symbols adorning the center and the four corners.

Everything in the tent spoke of her Apache heritage—the gathering baskets in one corner, the beaded moccasins, the clay bowls. Joseph was transported back to his childhood, back to a time when being Sioux caused him pride rather than shame, back to a time when he would have fought to the death to defend the name Hawk.

The Hawk. His father's spirit guide, his totem.

Surrounded by nature and the trappings of a once great nation, a long-buried pride floated to the surface, and he soared, as strong and fierce as the great bird of prey from which he took his name.

Callie touched his cheek, and in the moonlight spilling through the tent door he saw wonder in her face.

"I'm so glad you came," she whispered. Sighing, she settled against him, her body soft and yielding.

He traced her face with his fingertips, memorizing

every line. The poetry of his people filled his soul, and overflowed.

"Soft as the hart to the spring goes my heart to yours. I drink your sparkling waters, the nectar of the sweetest flowers, and I am content."

"That's beautiful," she said. With wanton abandon she lifted herself away from him and spread herself upon the blanket, her hair a velvet cloud and her legs a silken invitation.

"Drink my sparkling waters," she whispered.

Joseph seized the moment, for all too soon it would be gone. Yesterday would be a dream and tomorrow might not never come.

She was sweet and warm and moist, like strawberries ripened in the sun and eaten straight from the vine. He couldn't get enough of her. With lips and tongue he teased her, devoured her, and brought her once again to the edge of the precipice.

Arching high under his questing tongue, she caught fistfuls of blanket and held on so she wouldn't fall over.

But the delicious agony was too much to bear—for both of them.

"Joseph, Joseph!"

She screamed out her need, and Joseph lifted her up so that they faced each other, joined heart and body, her legs wrapped around his waist, her arms around his neck. The wind caught her cries and lifted them up toward the darkening sky where they merged with the stars.

Chapter Fifteen

When Joseph woke up, Callie was gone. He had hoped to wake up with her in his arms. He had hoped to make slow, gentle love to her, not merely for the beauty of it, but to make up to her for the savage mating of the night before.

His blood heated at the thought of her. So strong was his need, so hot was his passion that if she walked through the door he would have a hard time staying away from her.

Still, Joseph knew he had to show Callie that she was more to him than a sexual partner. If he couldn't tell her of his love, the least he could do was show her kindness, compassion and a tender regard.

He dressed quickly and went outside. Her horse was gone. Joseph's heart sank. What did that mean? With Callie, it could mean anything. She was not the kind of woman who gave herself lightly, and she was certainly not the kind of woman who cast principles to the four winds simply because Joseph had walked up her mountain and into her life.

Temporarily, he reminded himself. His stay on Callie's mountain was temporary.

He knelt beside the fire she'd built that morning. The ashes were cold. Callie had been gone a long time.

But where?

"Callie?" Joseph called her, softly at first, then with hands cupped to his mouth. "Callie!"

There was no answer, only the sound of squirrels chattering in the branches overhead and the sound of wind in the trees. Though she had taken her horse, Joseph walked the perimeters of the camp, venturing into the woods as far as he wanted to go on foot.

Back at camp, he went inside the tent. Her clothes were still there, as well as the gathering baskets, her blankets, her clay pots. She wouldn't leave without her things.

Or would she? As hot-tempered as she was hot-blooded, she would always be a woman full of surprises and contradictions.

There was only one thing left to do: get on his horse and find her. Joseph looked askance at the stallion. Thunderbolt tossed his head in a gesture of pure disdain.

"I guess it's just you and me, old boy."

Thunderbolt whinnied and pawed the ground. Joseph took a firm stand.

"Only one of us is going to come out a winner this time, and it's not going to be you."

The stallion accepted the bridle, but when Joseph put the saddle on his back, he kicked and bucked as if he meant business. Why had it been so easy when Callie's father did it?

Joseph felt foolish. From the looks of things, you'd

think he had never ridden a horse. Exactly the opposite was true. He'd had his own pony as a child, then in his teenage years he'd owned a horse that was the envy of his friends, a beautiful paint named Stargazer who won every race Joseph entered.

On Stargazer Joseph had felt ten feet tall. He remembered the feel of the wind in his hair and the sun on his face. He remembered the rich smells of spring, the greening grasses, the pungent scent of cedar trees, the pregnant earth ripe with flowers. He had ridden barebacked, leaning low over Stargazer's back, guiding the horse with knees and whispered commands.

Seized by inspiration, Joseph cast the saddle aside, then went inside the tent for one of Callie's blankets.

"Is this what you want, old boy?"

Docile, Thunderbolt accepted the blanket, and when Joseph leaped on his back, the stallion still stood at perfect attention. Joseph patted his neck.

"I should have known this is what you're accustomed to."

He had no idea which direction to go, but Thunderbolt had a few ideas of his own.

"I guess you've been here before, huh boy?"

Joseph gave the horse his head, and twenty minutes from camp he received his reward. He didn't have to draw in the reins, for the horse knew that no creature in his right mind, neither man nor beast, could resist the view. They came upon it suddenly, and it literally took Joseph's breath away.

A lake of the most impossible blue lay underneath a sky that looked as if it had been polished. Massive bluffs surrounded the lake, and a waterfall roared down one of the sheer rock faces. Ancient trees rose up to meet the sky, benevolent giants who guarded the secluded valley, and keeping watch over all was the sun.

As Joseph watched, sky and land and water merged into one sparkling jewel, and in its center was Callie Red Cloud.

She emerged from the falls, naked and glorious, and in one smooth move plunged into the sky-blue waters. With strong, sure strokes she swam the length of the lake, and when she walked ashore, she was so serene, so confident, Joseph could have sworn he was looking at a goddess.

His heart lifted, and with it his hands and his voice. In the ancient ways of his people, he paid homage to four beloved things above—the clouds, the sun, the clear sky, and He who lives in the clear sky.

The years fell away, and he was once again Sioux, deeply in love with the land and the woman who graced it.

She was worthy of adoration, of songs, of gifts. The wind stirred the cedars, and Joseph reached up and plucked cedar boughs, then pressed his knees into the stallion's side.

"Go like the wind. Callie waits."

Callie heard the thundering hooves and even before she saw the stallion, she knew its rider. She knew in her bones, in her blood, in her heart. She knew, and she waited.

When she looked up, Joseph filled her vision, blocking out the sun and the tall green grasses and the sweet blue waters that had cooled her hot skin. She knew other things, too, feelings so raw, so real they filled her up until there was room for nothing else, not rational thought, not plans, not even a future. Just the here and the now. Only the moment. Nothing else existed. Nothing else mattered.

Joseph's hair was long and dark, and he rode bareback. On the colorful blanket astride the powerful stallion, he was every inch Sioux.

Callie's heart thundered as loudly as the horse's hooves.

If only it were so. If only Joseph would acknowledge his heritage. If only...

Joseph drew the stallion to a halt. "I woke up and you were gone."

His face told stories so sweet she wanted to swoon. *I missed you,* it said. *I wanted you there by my side.*

"I often come here," she said. "To think and to meditate."

He swung down from the stallion and cupped her face. "What were you thinking of, Callie?"

His voice was soft, seductive, a full and complete acknowledgment of what they were to each other. The thing about Joseph that she loved was how he made her feel. Dignified. Worthy. Even naked, with the sun warming her skin, she felt like a queen clothed in the finest robes.

"I was thinking of you," she said.

Another man might have pressed for more, might have fished for compliments. Not Joseph. He didn't have to fish: he knew, and the knowing made his eyes gleam.

He ran his fingertips over her face, gathering droplets of moisture.

"Of us," she whispered.

"Yes," he said. "Of us."

Then he put his forefinger in her mouth, and she tasted the warm water of the lake and the sun on his skin and something else, something so powerful, so compelling, so appealing she could do nothing but sigh.

Boulders surrounded them, and the basin was full of rocks. Kneeling, Joseph laid cedar boughs upon the stone.

"A gift for you," he said.

She took his uplifted hand, and kneeling on the cedars she kissed him. The kiss was sweet and deep and tender, for now Callie knew what it was like to love this man.

Her kiss touched the part of him that was Sioux and unleashed the poetry in his soul. With his hands on her face and his lips only inches from hers, he sang to her of passion that tangled his roots with hers and of hearts planted deep in the breast of Mother Earth so that they grew so big they reached the Father Sky where he turned them into all the stars of the Milky Way.

When Joseph had finished, she whispered one word, "Hawk," and he knew she was calling him to love her, calling him to soar, calling him by name.

All the ancient ways came back to him, and he cast aside his clothes, then knelt before her once more, a noble savage with one fierce purpose: to claim his woman.

"There is an ancient dance for those who love," he said.

"Do we love, Joseph? Is that what we do?"

"Do you doubt it, Callie?"

He clasped both her hands and his eyes pierced her like arrows. She wet her lips with the tip of her tongue.

"No," she whispered. "After last night, how can I doubt that we love? My only doubt is that it will last."

Knowing that what she said was true, knowing that he would leave, he died a little inside.

"We have today." His eyes questioned her. *Is that enough?*

"Yes," she whispered.

She gazed deep into his eyes, and the moment crystalized. A breeze whispered secrets and a cardinal swooped so low he momentarily blotted out the sun.

"Teach me the ancient dance, Joseph."

"It is called the mirror dance. The lovers kneel facing each other, as we are doing now, then each one touches himself to show the other what he wants."

He pressed his palms hard against hers so he could feel her body as it heated up.

"Show me what you want, Callie."

"This," she said, cupping her breasts so that they were offered up to him, then slowly, ever so slowly she circled her thumbs around her nipples until they were hard as diamonds.

His eyes burned into hers as he reached out to mirror her action. She was rich and ripe in his hands, her flesh hot, her breasts heavy with desire. His thumbs circled, massaged, teased. Callie arched her back, lifting herself toward him, and her head fell back so that the long, lovely length of her throat was exposed to him.

Hunger lashed him and desire drove him to the brink of control. It took every bit of restraint he possessed not to press her back against the cedar boughs and drive into her as he had last night.

"And what else?" he asked.

She wet her finger with the tip of her tongue, then touched her hardened nipples.

"This," she said.

He wet his own fingers and massaged her. Afterward he slid her fingers into his mouth then guided her hands in a slow erotic massage over his own chest.

"More," she whispered.

Bending low, he drew her ripe breasts deep into his mouth and suckled until she was swaying and moaning like the north wind. Still, he kept his mouth on her, savoring, tasting, teasing. Driving her wild. Driving him mad.

And when he had finished he tasted the salt of his own

sweat. Facing him, Callie was as tightly wound as a piano wire. With eyes gleaming like twin stars, she touched herself intimately, erotically.

"Here," she whispered, and he bent to taste the sweet hot dampness of her.

She lifted her hips to give him better access, and he delved inside, exploring her deep, dark mysteries. Need clawed at him, and his heart pounded like war drums.

Trembling, he held back. Control was his gift to Callie.

He could feel her passion building, building, building, and when she exploded he caught her back to give her support. She wove her hands into his hair and lifted his face to hers. The kiss was openmouthed, deep and hot and hard.

She drew a long, trembling breath. "And you," she whispered. "Show me what you want."

His muscles so tight he could barely move, he touched himself. Her eyes riveted on his, Callie closed her hand around him, and then…magic. Joseph groaned like a giant redwood axed in its prime.

Without urging, she bent to take him in her mouth. Then, as if she'd read his mind, she whispered, "No more mirror dance. Just you and me, Hawk."

When he lowered her to the cedar boughs he was Hawk, strong and tender, and when he entered her he was Hawk, big and bold. And when he took up a slow, sweet rhythm, he was Hawk, soaring so high above Mother Earth that his wings touched the sun.

Soaring, dipping, diving, he carried her with him. The sun overhead warmed their skin, and the sun inside seared their hearts, melding them so tightly together that Joseph knew nothing could separate them. Not time, not distance, not even death.

There were no acrobatics, no calisthenics, no tricks, just

Hawk and Callie riding the sweet wild currents until they exploded and plunged back to the ground, back to the soft bough of cedars on the hard rocks.

He pressed her close, murmuring into her hair, "Sweet, so sweet, my love," while she wrapped her arms around him and held on as if she would never let go. Never. Neither in this lifetime nor the next.

And for a moment Joseph believed it might be so. For a moment he glimpsed a future for them and saw that it could be good.

Then Thunderbolt snorted and Callie sat up and the spell was broken.

"We're going to get a sunburn if we stay here like this," she said.

Sunburn was the least of his worries.

"We're doctors," he said. "We can cure ourselves."

The lights went out of her, and she looked deep into his eyes.

"Can we?" she whispered. "Can we cure ourselves, Joseph?"

If she had called him Hawk, he might have said, yes, anything is possible. But she had called him Joseph and so he told her the stark truth.

"I don't know," he said.

She turned her back to him and walked down to the lake to gather her clothes. If the truth weren't so heavy in him, he might have walked down after her so that they could cavort in the water.

Instead he lifted a bough and pressed it to his face, inhaling the sharp scent of cedar and the pungent scent of sex.

Callie, Callie, his heart cried. But he was stone, cold and silent.

"Joseph." She was already dressed when she called

him from the edge of the lake. "Thunderbolt will come if you whistle."

She swung onto her mount and waited for him, distant and unattainable.

Chapter Sixteen

Back at camp she dismounted then tossed him a fishing pole.

"Around here you work for your dinner," she said.

How long will you stay? she wanted to say.

"My mother always taught me that work is good for the soul," he said.

I don't ever want to leave you, he wanted to say.

"Is she still living?" she asked.

Can you ever truly love again? she wanted to ask.

"Yes, in the Black Hills of South Dakota."

I love you, he wanted to say.

Sometimes when skirting around the real issues, one runs out of things to say. That's what happened to Callie and Joseph. He retreated into that waiting stillness she knew so well, and she busied herself getting their fishing gear together.

Her body was still heavy with him. His scent was on

her skin. And yet she felt as if they had suddenly become strangers.

If they were in a hospital she would know what to say. If they were fighting a hot virus, she would know what to do.

But they were in a camp in the mountains, and she had no experience in dealing with a love that was destined to end. She had no experience with love. Period.

Her relationships had been few and far between, and then only the kind where two people merged for a short while, like rivers whose paths crossed, then went their separate ways without leaving behind a single ripple to show they had ever met.

She was not prepared for the kind of soul-searing pain that could squeeze a heart in two. She was not prepared for the kind of loneliness that would swallow you up. She was not prepared to talk about things that would lead to goodbye.

And so she picked up her fishing pole and went to the stream. Actually, she stalked. She'd always done that when she got mad. She used to stomp around so hard Eric told her she sounded like a whole posse. That was in the days when he glued himself to the television set every afternoon to watch an old Western starring Gene Autry or Roy Rogers, or Callie's favorite, the Lone Ranger.

That's who she felt like right now. The Lone Ranger. All of a sudden she was boiling mad. She knew where the anger came from, of course. It was a protective shield against pain.

What right did Joseph have to come riding into her life? What right did he have to waltz into her camp and seduce her? Who did he think he was?

Furious now, she drew back her pole and cast with such force the line snagged a tree branch across the stream.

"Shoot, look at that."

She gave a small tug, and when that didn't work she pulled with all her might. She was so mad she didn't even hear Joseph come up behind her.

"Here." He circled her with his arms, and covered her hands with his. "Let me help with that."

She jabbed him in the ribs with her elbows. Hard.

"Haven't you done enough already?"

A great silence came over him. For a moment, he held on to her hands, and then he stepped back.

Good, she thought. She didn't need him. Not for fishing, not for sex, not for anything.

She could feel him, standing a few feet behind her, and darned if she didn't want to turn around, put her hands on his face and say, I'm sorry.

Callie resisted the impulse. What did she have to be sorry about? He was the one who had come here and messed up everything. She'd been perfectly content until he showed up. Hadn't she? And now, look at her. She couldn't even cast a fishing line.

She could feel his body heat. She could hear him breathing back there.

"Go away and leave me alone," she said.

She gave the pole a vicious jerk. The branch bent far out over the water, then sprang back, taking her pole with it.

Hands on her hips, she whirled on Joseph. "Now, see what you've done."

He was so still, and his eyes... The look in them shook her very soul.

Without a word he waded into the stream, clothes, boots and all. Let him get wet. What did she care? The water became knee deep, then thigh deep, then waist deep.

When it got up to his chest, Callie could no longer stand to be quiet.

"Come back here. What are you doing?"

Solemn as a judge, he turned around to face her. "I'm fixing the mess I made."

Any other man would have looked ridiculous standing in the middle of a stream fully clothed, but Joseph was one of those men who wore dignity like a second skin. Callie couldn't stay mad at him. To make matters worse, she wanted him.

That was all it took, one look, and passion rode her so hard she nearly swooned. She clamped down hard on her emotions, and tried for anger once more.

"You just stop right there. I'll get it."

He called her bluff. "By all means, be my guest."

Callie didn't hesitate an instant. It wouldn't be the first time she'd ever gone swimming with clothes on. She kicked off her shoes and waded in.

She marched straight toward Joseph. The water rose quickly to her waist, but she plowed ahead, straight toward him. His silence goaded her.

"It's my pole," she said.

Something flickered in his eyes. Something dangerous.

"It certainly is," he said.

Callie shivered but not from the chill. Joseph Swift Hawk was not talking about fishing.

The look in his eyes might have caused the faint of heart to retreat, but Callie had never been faint of heart. Boldly, she advanced. The water lapped at her breasts, and watching, Joseph didn't try to disguise his feelings.

Callie meant to swim straight past him. She meant to turn her focus to the tangled fishing line. She meant to show him that she didn't need anybody. But in the end she couldn't. She could no more swim past him than she could fly.

"Callie." His voice was soft, seductive, and when he reached for her hand she didn't fight him.

He pulled her swiftly toward him and crushed her against his chest. Pressed fully against him, wet and slick and hungry, she could feel every muscle in his body, every sinew, every hard ridge.

"Callie..."

Desire stormed them, and they went wild. Shirts drifted downstream, pants floated on the water, but they didn't notice. Legs and arms tangled, they came together like two thunderclouds. Heaving and panting, they devoured each other.

And when it was over, when their passion was finally spent, she bowed her head on his chest and cried.

He wove his hands through her thick wet hair, stroking, soothing.

"Cry it out, Callie."

She didn't need his permission to cry, but she was glad he gave it. Most men hated a woman's tears. She was glad he wasn't that kind of man.

She cried for Ricky, she cried for Joseph, she cried for herself. She cried for missed chances and lost opportunities and closed doors. She cried over sickness and loneliness and crippling old age. Clinging to him, she cried over war, famine, death. She cried for everything she could think of.

And he held her the entire time, comforting with soft murmuring and tender touches. How could she bear to lose this man?

When her sobs subsided, he carried her to the bank and lay down facing her on the soft earth.

"It's time to talk, Callie."

"Yes." She wiped her face with the back of her hand. "I know."

"I should have talked when I first came here instead of..."

"Shhh." She put her hand over his mouth. "Don't say it. Don't ever be sorry."

"Are you sorry, Callie?"

"No. Not one bit. I have no regrets. If you rode into my camp again just the way you did last night I would do the same thing."

"Has it been only one night? It seems like years."

He didn't have to explain, for she felt exactly the same way, as if they had always been lovers, as if they had always known each other, not merely in this life but through the centuries. His face was as familiar to her as her own. His body was so much a part of her, that she couldn't tell where hers left off and his began.

"Callie, I came to you because I had no choice. We started something in Houston that had to be finished."

"Is it finished, then?"

"No." He touched her cheek, tenderly, briefly. "I'm not sure it will ever be finished."

"Nor am I."

His eyes were dark and deep. A woman could get lost in them, and Callie did. They lay facing each other, not touching, not moving, not speaking while the wind and sun moved over them.

He was the first to move. Reaching out, he traced her lips with the tip of his forefinger.

"If I thought it would work...if I thought I could live with the terror of watching you around the hot viruses...if I thought you wouldn't grow to hate me because I've renounced my Sioux name..."

If he hadn't hesitated, Callie might have let him continue talking. And if he had, he might have said, *I love you no matter what, we'll work it out.*

That hesitation, that small doubt moved her to action. She put her hand over his mouth again.

"Shhh, don't say anything else. You're right. It would never work."

Would it? Now she would never know.

"Sometimes, being right is the most painful thing in the world."

"You get over pain. What you don't get over is the tragic mistakes. They have a way of haunting you forever."

She ought to know. Already she could see the tragedy in their saying goodbye. Were they doing the right thing? Would she ever love again? And even if she did, would she ever love as deeply, as surely, as strongly? The questions would haunt her forever.

He knew, too. She could see it in his eyes.

"I can only stay a little while longer, Callie. Perhaps a few more days."

"Don't tell me. I don't want to know." She wove her hands through his hair and pulled him close for a long and tender kiss. "When the time comes, leave the way you came, Joseph, without warning."

"You want me to leave without saying goodbye." It was not a question; it was a statement.

"Every time we make love, we're saying goodbye," she said.

"Then perhaps we shouldn't make love."

A smile played around his lips, and she was glad to lighten the mood.

"Don't you dare stop."

"Not even long enough for food? I'm starved."

"So am I. Let's eat."

He got a wicked gleam in his eye. Callie put her hand on his chest and gave a slight push.

"I'm talking about eating fish," she said.

"So am I...eventually."

They ended up eating pork and beans straight from the can...eventually.

His first kiss was so tender it broke her heart. His second was so gentle it moved her to tears. His third was so soft it rearranged her world.

They lay together on the cushion of grass kissing, and that was all. No sharp stabs of desire. No burning passion. No explosive mating. Just Callie and Hawk kissing as if their lives depended on it.

And perhaps they did. Perhaps both of them needed this sweet interlude to sustain them in the empty days ahead.

Holding each other close, they kissed until their hearts glowed and their skin felt warm to the touch. And then they left the stream and went into camp where they put on robes then sat cross-legged on an Indian blanket, eating pork and beans from the same can.

"This may be the best meal I've had in a while," he said.

Callie laughed. "It's the *only* meal you've had in a while."

"I had other things on my mind," he said. "I suppose we'd starve to death if we lived with each other."

Folding his hands behind his head, Joseph leaned back against a tree trunk and Callie imagined what it would be like to sit beside him every evening after supper.

"What do you do in the evenings?" she said.

"Read, play the guitar, take long walks through the hills, listen to great blues, watch old movies on TV." He smiled. "Most people find me boring."

"I don't," she said.

"What do you do, Callie?"

"Read, take long walks through the mountains, listen to great blues, watch old movies on TV." They both laughed. "Everything except play the guitar. Or sometimes I ride." His eyes gleamed with devilment. "Horses," she added.

An owl called from deep in the woods, and overhead the first star of the evening lit the sky. Joseph unfolded his long legs, stood up and reached for her hand.

"This evening I have another mount in mind for you."

Underlying his soft-spoken invitation was a note of urgency that made Callie lose her breath. She took his hand and let him lead her into the tent.

"In Sheridan, Wyoming, there is an ancient stone structure rising ten thousand feet above the earth with spokes running outward and the skull of a buffalo lying in the center, facing the sun. It's called the medicine wheel."

"Yes," she whispered, for she'd been there to see this sacred symbol of the Native Americans. And she knew its significance, but she kept quiet, for it thrilled her to see Joseph caught up in the heritage he insisted he had denied.

"Everything goes in a circle," he continued, "and that circle is sacred, filled with mystery and power."

He spread her most colorful blanket upon the tent floor and drew her down with him. Then he untied her robe and peeled it from her shoulders. It slid to the floor, and his tongue traced its path, across her throat, along her shoulder, down the length of her arm all the way to her fingertips.

Closing her eyes, she gave herself up to the glory of his touch.

"Nature completes the circle every day, starting with the rising of the sun and ending with the rising of the new moon," he said.

He cast off his robe, then gently pressed her back against the blanket. Kneeling over her, he trailed his tongue in a white-hot line from her breasts to her navel.

"From birth to death to rebirth man goes in the sacred circle, and if he's very lucky he can occasionally capture some of the mystery and the power."

He moved his tongue lower, ever lower, until at last he found what he sought. Overcome by sensation, Callie could do nothing more than moan. Joseph interrupted her moans with a kiss that seared her soul.

"The mystery and power are here, Callie," he whispered. "On the medicine wheel."

He lay beside her, and she took him in her mouth while his tongue searched for sweet mysteries.

"We never did fish," she said when they woke up the next morning.

"I had better things to do." His smile was teasing. "What about you?"

"Yes, but I think we'll both get tired of eating pork and beans."

"All right, then. Let's untangle your line and go fishing."

Instead of wading the water, they hiked upstream to a bridge, then hiked back down to the point where Callie's fishing line was tangled high in a giant oak tree. Joseph didn't relish the idea of climbing the tree, not at his age. In fact, he wasn't even sure he could still climb a tree, but he wasn't about to tell that to Callie. He had his pride.

"Boost me up," she said, "and I'll get it."

"No. I'll do it."

He didn't fool her for a minute. Her amusement started as a smile and ended in full-fledged laughter.

"I don't see what's so funny," he said.

"You should have seen your face when you said you'd climb that tree."

"I will climb that tree. I used to do it all the time."

"When?"

"When I was a child."

"And how long ago was that?"

"Callie Red Cloud, are you asking my age?"

"Yes."

Nobody could ever accuse Callie of being shy, he thought.

And that was one of the things he loved most about her—her boldness.

"Didn't you do your research? I'm surprised you don't already know."

"Does all this beating around the bush mean you're not going to tell me?"

"Age doesn't matter to me. Does it to you?"

"Yes." She burst into laughter again. "I'm talking about tree climbing. I need to know your age so I'll know if you're too old to climb that tree."

"Did I say anything?"

"No, but your face did. How old are you?"

"Forty, and right now I feel every minute of it."

"Boost me up," she said.

"What?"

"Give me a boost. I'm going up that tree."

He had visions of Callie tumbling down, and him trying to get her out of the mountains on a makeshift stretcher.

"I can't let you do that," he said.

"Why not?"

"What if you fall and break your neck?"

"Are you always such a worrywart?"

"Yes."

"Oh, Lord."

"Does that mean you're not going to sleep with me anymore?" Now it was his turn to tease.

"Did we sleep?"

"Not much. I'm still not too old for that."

"You're certainly not."

The way she said it, soft and seductive, made his blood hot, and he knew that it would be a long while before either of them climbed the tree.

Chapter Seventeen

They had fish for supper. Callie caught two, Joseph caught one, and he built a campfire where they grilled their catch to perfection.

He decided *perfection* was a good word to describe their day. When they finally got around to untangling her line, he'd given her a boost up the tree, and it hadn't surprised him one bit that Callie climbed a tree the way she did everything else, with an ease that made all his fears seem foolish.

Afterward they'd hiked high into the mountains, following the meandering stream to a point where it widened and deepened in the midst of towering evergreens. He hadn't fished since he was a child, and he'd forgotten how relaxing it could be. They'd talked some, lighthearted banter mostly, and laughed a lot.

He could almost believe they could stay on the White

Mountains forever, isolated and insulated, the real world faded into nothingness.

It was not to be so. Already he felt the pull of reality.

"A meal fit for a king," Callie said as she took the fish off the fire.

"And his queen." Joseph sniffed the good aroma. "Hmm, delicious."

"I have a surprise for you," she said.

"What is it?"

He loved to hear her laugh. It was one of the things he would remember most. He knew exactly how it would be: he would be lying in bed with a breeze stirring the curtains at the casement window, and he would hear Callie's laughter, suddenly and without warning.

Even now, just thinking how it would be, he felt as if a giant hand were squeezing his chest. The reality of it would be almost unbearable.

"Joseph?" Her voice brought him back to the present. "What happened? You vanished."

"Just thinking."

Almost as if she'd read his mind, she went still and watchful, and he could see pain deep in her eyes. She knew. Callie knew that he would be leaving.

He wanted to go to her and take her in his arms and comfort her, but what was there to say? Words wouldn't ease the hurt. He knew that.

And she had made it clear she didn't want goodbyes.

Mentally he shrugged off the dark mood. "So, what is your wonderful surprise?"

Callie seized the chance to lighten the mood. "If I told you it wouldn't be a surprise. Wait right here."

She vanished inside the tent and returned with a bottle of wine.

"I've been saving this for a special occasion," she said.

"All we need is music. I wish you had brought your guitar."

"I have a little surprise of my own." He went into the tent and got his harmonica out of his backpack. "Will this do?"

"You never cease to amaze me. Is there no end to your talents?"

"Not when I'm with you, Callie."

She kissed him softly on the lips, then leaned back, smiling.

"Let's eat first," she said.

She spread a blanket, and they sat close, feeding each other bites of fish. Then afterward she lay with her head in his lap while he played the harmonica, mostly blues.

Callie's favorite was an old Eubie Blake, Noble Sissle song called "Gee, I Wish I Had Someone to Rock Me in the Cradle of Love."

She made him play it twice, and while he played the stars came out one by one and a full moon hung overhead, so close it looked as if it were snagged in the branches of the tree.

A perfect night for lovers. A perfect night for romance. A perfect night for saying goodbye.

Joseph looked down at Callie's beautiful face, and it was like no other to him, special in ways he couldn't begin to describe. In the moonlight she looked like something he might have dreamed.

In fact, this entire idyll in the mountains had a surreal quality, as if any moment he might awaken to find himself in his own bed with nothing more than a fleeting memory of a dream too wonderful to be true.

"Star light, star bright," Callie said. "When I was little I used to wish upon a star."

"Did all your wishes come true, Callie?"

"All of them," she whispered.

Joseph laid down his harmonica, then picked her up and carried her inside their tent. She put her hands on her buttons, but he covered them with his own.

"Let me," he said.

He unveiled her slowly, memorizing every line, every curve, every hollow. And then with hands and lips and tongue he adored her, trailing his fingertips down the length of her body from throat to hip, following that erotic path with lips and tongue.

Her pulse beat wildly. He could feel it in the lovely indention at the base of neck. With his lips pressed against her throat, he inhaled her scent. Always, she smelled of flowers, some light perfume he'd seen her pat into soft, secret places in the early morning. Her skin had its own fragrance, too, an exotic, erotic musk that he would remember as long as he lived.

Remember and yearn for.

The soft mounds of her breasts claimed his attention, and he smothered his face between them, then he took one dusky rose tip deep into his mouth and suckled until Callie was moaning and writhing beneath him.

Her response fanned the flames that already threatened to consume him, but he reined himself under control. Tonight was goodbye. He had to make it last a lifetime.

She wove her hands in his hair, holding him tightly against her breasts, and he knew that he could spend an eternity there and never tire, never get enough.

What would it be like to turn in his bed at night and find this woman at his side? What would it be like to watch his seed grow in her womb? What would it be like to see his son cradled in her arms suckling these same rosy nipples he found so exciting?

It would be paradise. But it was lost to him.

He had only this night.

With lips and tongue he explored every inch of her, rediscovering every sensitive spot on her body. He was filled with wonder at the chemistry between them, at the way each touch brought an instant response from her, at the way her heart matched the runaway rhythm of his own.

She urged him on with soft murmurings and sweet cries, and when at last he entered her, he knew that what they had together was not merely passion, not merely desire: it was love.

Wrapped tightly in her arms, Joseph rocked her gently while the moon traveled through the night sky. And before the stars began to fade, he took her on that final wild ride to sweet release.

Slack and damp, she clung to him. And when she spoke his name, he had to lean close to hear.

"Joseph," she whispered. "Joseph, my love."

So full he couldn't speak, he brushed her damp hair from her forehead, and by the time he thought how to reply she was fast asleep. He held her in his arms, watching her sleep until the first faint fingers of dawn crept across the sky, and then he dressed quietly, strapped on his backpack and rode away.

"Don't look back," he told himself. "Don't look back." For he knew if he did, he could never leave.

Even before she opened her eyes, Callie knew Joseph was gone. She'd known when they were making love that it would be their last time.

She lay perfectly still, knowing if she moved she would shatter into a million pieces. All the things she might have said played through her mind. All the things she could have done differently haunted her.

And yet…

None of it would have made the least bit of difference. Fate brought them together, and fate tore them apart.

"What is meant to be will be," her grandmother used to tell her. "The universe has its own time."

Joseph's essence was still in the tent. She could smell him, feel him, hear him, see him. She wrapped her arms around herself as if he were still there, as if she could feel his skin pressing against hers.

Then she closed her eyes and replayed every touch, every kiss, every beautiful moment they had spent together since they first met. The tears were in her heart, in her throat, but she didn't dare let them out. If she started crying she might never stop.

"I will remember you, Joseph," she whispered. "Always."

With that declaration, she got up and went outside to greet the dawn. His horse was gone, as she'd known it would be. The blanket they had spread beside the fire last night was still there, and on it was Joseph's harmonica.

Callie picked it up and pressed it to her lips.

Joseph hadn't meant to look back, but he couldn't help himself. High on a ridge overlooking Callie's camp he sat on his horse watching. When she came out from the tent it took every ounce of restraint he possessed not to race to her side.

She was walking straight and tall, head up, chin out.

Callie would be fine. He knew that. But the knowledge gave him no relief.

When Callie picked up his harmonica and pressed it to her lips, loss sliced his heart. Rooted to the spot he watched her slip the harmonica in her pocket, then bridle her horse and ride in the direction of the lake.

He watched until she disappeared into the forest.

"Goodbye, my love," he whispered, and then he turned his stallion to the path that led down the mountain.

Callie was not one to wallow in pain. Never had been, never would be.

When she got to the lake she shucked her clothes and swam until she was exhausted. Then she spread her blanket on the ground and lay with her eyes tightly shut and the sun beating down on her. It was her way of giving herself over to the universe and allowing nature to heal her.

She didn't know how long she lay there, one hour, two. It didn't matter. At last a calmness and certainty settled over her, and she got up, broke camp and rode down the mountain.

"Hello, Dad."

She dismounted and kissed him on the cheek. She looked thinner than when she'd left. Calder hugged her a long time. He pulled back to study her face. Close up he could see the strain around her eyes and lips.

"Are you all right, Daughter?"

"Yes." Her chin came up. "Why wouldn't I be?"

"When I got up this morning, Thunderbolt was in his stall."

"Yes. Joseph has gone."

Her face told him nothing, but her eyes made him want

to take Joseph by the nape and shake him. If Calder were younger he'd do it, too.

"Does Mom know?" Callie said.

"I haven't told her. I figure you'll let us know whatever we need to."

"Thanks, Dad." She kissed his cheek again. "I need to talk to you about something very important."

"Let me tell Betty."

Calder went back inside to tell the receptionist that he was leaving for the rest of the day.

He took Callie's arm, and together they walked back to the house. There was a gazebo out back, half hidden from the main house by a thick hedge of pink roses. When her father had built the thing twenty years ago he'd meant it to be a romantic hideaway for Ellen and himself, but over the years it had turned into the perfect place to take his children when they needed a heart-to-heart talk.

The gazebo was bigger than most. It was filled with white wicker furniture with thick yellow cotton canvas cushions. Calder sat in the rocking chair.

Callie didn't sit down, but perched against the railing. Calder rocked and waited.

"I've decided to leave the center and come home to practice with you," she said.

Just like that. For years Calder had longed to hear those words, and now that she'd said them he was surprised at how he felt: off balance, like a kite with a shortened tail, trying to catch a current in order to stay aloft.

"Are you sure?" he said.

"Yes, I'm sure."

No hesitation. That was good. And yet, there was the matter of Joseph Swift. He didn't like to think that a daughter of his would tuck tail and run home because of a broken heart.

"What changed your mind?" he said.

"This has nothing to do with Joseph Swift." Callie was always good at knowing what Calder was thinking. "I didn't even discuss it with him."

"If you had told him, would it have made a difference?"

"I don't know. Maybe." She jumped up and began to pace. "I didn't want my job to be a factor with Joseph, Dad. Just as I didn't want Ricky to be a factor."

"Who's Ricky?"

Callie sat cross-legged on the floor and told him all about the little boy who had survived the *arbo* virus and how she'd tried to adopt him.

"I'm going back to Texas, Dad, to try again."

"When?"

"After I talk to Ron. I have to fly back to Atlanta and resign face-to-face. I owe him that much."

Calder rocked and felt the wind on his face. His daughter was coming home and he could slide safely into old age knowing that his people would continue to have the best of medical care. He would ride into the mountain tomorrow in the ancient way and pay homage to four Beloved Things Above for this remarkable gift.

The thought of having another grandchild pleased him, too. He reached for his daughter's hand.

"Today, you've made me very happy."

"I'm glad."

Calder took her hand. "Let's go inside and tell your mother. Maybe this news will soften her up."

Ellen was in her sewing room bent over a christening dress she was making for Eric's baby. When she saw Calder, she put her work in the sewing basket and faced him, arms akimbo.

"I have a bone to pick with you, Calder Red Cloud."

"Better tell her now." Calder said to Callie.

"Tell me what?" Ellen asked.

"About your new grandson." Calder blurted.

Ellen's mouth dropped open. Calder looked triumphant, and Callie began to laugh. Leave it to her father to take charge.

"I'll leave you to explain that, Dad. I have some packing to do."

Chapter Eighteen

Ron Messenger had a habit of polishing his glasses when he was disturbed. Callie sat in a stiff-backed chair and watched. He had taken the news of her leaving better than she had expected. But he was still rubbing his glasses, not looking at her, and she knew this meeting was not over. Not by a long shot.

"I'm not going to try to talk you out of this, Callie, because I know you didn't make this decision lightly."

"Thank you, Ron."

"You know how much I hate to lose you. You're the best virologist the center has."

"Your respect means a lot to me."

He smiled. "You know I'm buttering you up for a reason."

"I could feel it coming. What do you want, Ron? One more field trip? One more week? A pound of flesh?"

"None of the above." He slid his glasses on and peered

at her over the tops. "Remember that conference we talked about six months ago?"

"The one in D.C.?"

"Yes. It's in two weeks, and I'd like you to go with Peg to show her the ropes."

"Can't you send Jim? He would be a wonderful delegate." Jim had been at the center two years longer than Callie. His nickname was Old Reliable.

"Didn't Peg tell you? Jim's leaving tomorrow for Arizona."

"Not another outbreak?"

"No, just a little backup for the doctors out there. They've got an unidentified virus that's causing some concern."

"What about you, Ron? You used to go to all these conferences."

"Can't. Sandra's family is coming to town. Do this one last thing for me, Callie. That's all I ask."

Ron was not only her boss, he was her mentor and friend. How could Callie refuse?

"Of course, I'll do it, Ron."

He stood up and put his arm around her shoulder. "I'm going to miss you, Callie."

"I'll miss you, too, Ron," she said.

He kissed her cheek. "I'll be pulling for you. And if I need to fly down to Houston and kick some butt, I'll do that, too."

That evening Callie sat on the redwood deck recounting the day's events to Peg. Mike was in the kitchen working his magic on three big steaks he planned to grill.

"I'm going back to Houston tomorrow to talk with Miss Rayborn again about Ricky."

"If she's got a lick of sense she'll let you have that

kid. I can't think of anybody who would make a better mother than you...except me, of course." Peg poured herself another glass of tea, then leaned against the deck railing. "I'm envious, you know."

"About Ricky? About the job?"

"About both, I guess." She pressed the cold glass to her hot cheek. "Ever since I got back from Houston, Mike's been after me to quit. He was scared to death when he saw what all was happening out there."

Callie remembered her own fear when she saw Joseph shot.

"Who can blame him? It was frightening."

"Yeah, but that's not all. He wants to start a family."

"What about you?"

Peg blushed. "I'll tell you a little secret." She glanced to the kitchen to be sure Mike was still occupied, then leaned closer to whisper. "Last night I didn't use anything. When we discovered it, it was too late. I told Mike I forgot, but I don't think I did, not really. Somewhere in this voluptuous body of mine beats the heart of a woman who longs to be cookie chairman in kindergarten."

"Lord, Callie, I envy you." She sighed.

Mike came through the door holding a platter of steaks, marinated and ready for the grill. When he passed his wife, he leaned over and gave her a little squeeze around the waist.

Callie thought about the mountainside camp, about waking up to find Joseph leaning on one elbow watching her sleep, about the way he would kiss her softly and whisper, Wake up sleepyhead so we can greet the new dawn properly.

I envy you, Callie thought, but she didn't say it. Instead she smiled while Mike put the steaks on the grill.

"I hope you two are hungry," he said.

"I don't know about Callie, but I'm starved." Peg put her arms around her husband from behind, then winked at Callie.

"I am, too," Callie said, but she wasn't talking about steak.

Joseph's first sight of his homeland in three years caused him to pull his rented car off the road and simply stare.

The ancient Sioux considered the Black Hills to be the center of the universe, a place of spirits and holy matters. Joseph's ancestors used to go up into the hills alone to pray to the Great Spirit and await visions. Spirit quests, they were called, and all the great Sioux warriors claimed their power from these solitary journeys that combined prayer and fasting.

Sitting Bull. Crazy Horse. Joseph knew the names of them all. His mother had told him. She used to spend hours in front of the fire at night telling the myths and legends, trying to keep the great Sioux spirit alive.

When had it all died? When he was thirteen and hiding in the stall in the boys' bathroom, or when he'd entered college and come face-to-face with prejudice?

Nobody expected the Native American to amount to anything those days. In particular, they didn't expect one young Sioux fresh off the reservation to have the unmitigated gall to try for medical school.

Though Joseph had dropped Hawk from his name when he'd discovered his father's betrayal, there was no way he could change the color of his skin, his hair, his eyes. Still, it had been easier to call himself *Swift*.

And over the years he'd begun to think of himself that way, Joseph Swift, a self-made man without a past.

But when he returned to the Black Hills, Paha Sapa,

the ancient Sioux called them, he could no longer deny his heritage. There it was, spread before him in all its grandeur: the land the Sioux had prized for its beauty and spirituality—and others had prized for its gold.

"And that, folks, is how the West was lost," Joseph said.

He pulled back onto the road, and within an hour he was parking in front of his mother's house, a modest bungalow differentiated from the others on the street only by the yard. His mother had a green thumb, and in the summer and spring her yard rioted with color and scent.

Joseph sat for a while appreciating the beauty before he started toward the door.

He rang the bell, and when Sarah saw him, she stood with her hand over her heart, speechless.

"Hello, Mom," he said.

Suddenly Sarah became a whirlwind of activity, hugging, laughing, crying, sweeping wide the door, tidying the living room. Finally she wore herself out, and simply sat on the sofa staring at him.

"I can't believe it's really you."

"It's me, Mom."

Guilt stabbed Joseph. In the three years since he'd last seen her, Sarah's hair had gone from black shot through with gray to purest white. Wrinkles he didn't remember now creased her cheeks, and she was bent like an old willow loaded down with branches. These were changes you couldn't see in weekly phone calls home.

"I saw you on television down in Houston," she said. "You look thin."

Maybe he was. He hadn't eaten much in the mountainside camp. At the thought of Callie, pain sliced through him, sharp as knives.

Would it ever ease? Would the day ever come when he didn't think of her, want her, need her?

Need. The thought had come unbidden, and Joseph cast it away as if it were a rattlesnake. He didn't need anyone. A man living alone can't afford to need anybody.

"I have a casserole in the oven. Your favorite." Sarah pressed her hand over her heart.

"I should have called, but I wanted to surprise you."

Sarah reached for his hand, then tilted her head back so she could study his face.

"Something troubles you, Joseph." She didn't ask what it was.

"How is everything with you, Mom?"

"Retirement is boring. I miss the kids." After she'd left medical school, Sarah taught science in elementary school. "But I keep busy—gardening, cooking, doing my beadwork."

Sarah left the sofa to get an intricately beaded bag from her sewing basket. It was functional, but it was also art. Joseph noticed the price tag she'd attached.

"You could get three times that much," he said.

"I do this for pleasure, not money. Greed corrupts."

Joseph smiled. Sarah Brave Crow never changed. Until the day she died, she would still be teaching.

They ate the casserole, then afterward sat on the front porch to watch the moon and listen to the songs of the night creatures. Afterward, he slept in the bed of his youth. Sarah had never changed his room. It still had all his soccer trophies on the shelves, his posters of baseball heroes on the walls, and his collection of rocks from the Black Hills.

He had his first peaceful night's sleep in many years, and when he woke up he told his mother about Callie.

"Do you love her, Joseph?"

Joseph couldn't answer her. Love had not been a part of his vocabulary for years.

She left him sitting at the breakfast table, and when she came back she was carrying a sacred pipe and a small round stone.

"Do you remember the legend of the White Buffalo Woman?" his mother asked.

"I haven't thought of it in a long time."

Sarah ran her hands over the bowl of the pipe, carved in red stone, and when she spoke she reverted to a singsong cadence that mesmerized.

"The bowl of the pipe is your Mother and your Grandmother, the Earth, and the carving is a buffalo calf who represents all the four-legged creatures who walk upon Mother Earth. The wooden stem represents all things that grow upon her.

"The twelve feathers hanging from the pipe are from Wanbli Galeshka, the Spotted Eagle, and they are all the winged of the air."

The past pulled at him, and Joseph fought the urge to bolt. But he could never be rude to his mother, so he clenched his jaw and waited.

"When you smoke this pipe you are joined to all things and all people on Mother Earth, and when you pray they all send their voices to Wakan Tanka, the Great Spirit."

Swaying, Sarah closed her eyes, and Joseph got caught up in her vision. He could almost see the White Buffalo Woman storming across the plains, holding aloft the sacred pipe and the smooth round stone, red as Mother Earth and the new dawn that comes from Father Sky.

She opened her eyes and pressed the pipe and the stone into Joseph's hand.

"You are bound to all your relatives, Joseph, whether you want to be or not."

"I can't take these."

"I've saved them for you until you are ready." Sarah gently closed his hand around the sacred objects. "You are ready, my son."

Chapter Nineteen

Jenine Rayborn was not making things easy for Callie. Not that Callie expected any favors. She hadn't even expected the second interview with Jenine to be particularly comfortable. What she had expected was that Jenine would show a little enthusiasm for Callie's adoption quest. After all, if it hadn't been for Callie, Ricky wouldn't even be alive.

Joseph helped, too, of course. And Peg.

Still, Callie felt that she deserved an edge, and finally she told Jenine so.

"Miss Rayborn, I know you're trying to ensure that Ricky has the best possible home, but don't you think I deserve a little extra consideration here? If it weren't for me and my colleagues, Ricky wouldn't even be here."

"I'm well aware of that, Dr. Red Cloud."

Jenine picked up the letter from Ron vouching for Callie's character and verifying that she was, indeed, no longer employed by the Center for Disease Control. In other words, Callie had removed herself from that danger.

The minutes crept by, and at last Jenine laid aside the papers.

"Dr. Red Cloud, I'm well aware of your expertise in medicine. What I'm not aware of is your expertise in child rearing."

"Like all first-time mothers, I come to the job with no experience," Callie told her. "But I was brought up with love, and I know the importance of love in the mother-child relationship."

Jenine pursed her lips. "And there will be no father?"

Callie wanted to scream. "I think I've already made that clear. There will be no father."

"I don't mean to make this hard for you, Dr. Red Cloud, but we've already made two mistakes with Ricky. We can't afford to make a third. It's not good for the child to keep shuffling him around."

"I understand."

"This is going to take a while. We'll have to do an on-site visit, see what kind of home you'll be providing, what kind of hours you'll be working." She looked at Callie over the top of her glasses. "After all, you will still be practicing medicine."

"The clinic setting is vastly different from private practice where I would be associated with a hospital. It's almost like having a nine-to-five job, expect that I would take turns with Dr. Brenner being on call for emergencies."

"I understand."

Jenine came around her desk and took Callie's arm. "I know you would like for me to tell you yes today, but we have to work within strict guidelines, and then sometimes we still make mistakes. I don't want to make a mistake with this one. Ricky's already been through too much.''

''I agree,'' Callie said.

''This is going to take a few weeks, probably. Meantime, why don't you go down and visit Ricky? He's excited about seeing you again.''

Jenine smiled, and it was the first positive sign Callie had seen. She ducked into the ladies' room, more to get herself under control than to freshen up. Ricky didn't care a whit about how she looked.

Callie combed her hair, then pulled a lavender scented towelette from her bag and wiped her face.

''There,'' she said. ''That's better.''

Her hand was on the doorknob when instinct screamed at her, *Caution. Danger.*

Callie cracked the door open and peered out. Joseph was striding down the hall, big as life and twice as heartbreaking.

Her heart beating like a trip-hammer, Callie eased the door shut.

Safe.

But was she? Joseph was only a few feet away, and she had to anchor herself to the washbasin to keep from racing toward him like some lovesick puppy.

''I probably should have called ahead,'' she heard him say.

''No problem.'' *Jenine. Perky as a teenager.* ''Ricky will be thrilled to see you.''

Don't say it, Callie prayed. *Don't tell him I'm here.*

''You haven't found a home for him yet?'' Joseph asked.

''Not yet, but we're still trying.''

Oh, God. Would she tell Joseph about Callie's attempt to adopt?

Please, God, no, Callie prayed. Love couldn't be contingent on a job, a child.

Could it be contingent on a heritage?

She quickly pushed that thought aside. Their voices were fading. Callie risked pushing the door open an inch so she could hear.

"What happened with the last family?"

"Ricky ran away."

"Poor little guy."

"I know. If we don't find a home for him soon, I'm afraid he may end up as one of those hard cases, the ones nobody will take."

Not if I have anything to do with it, Callie thought.

"I wish things could be different," Joseph said.

Callie heard despair mixed with poignance in his voice, and she wanted to run after him, calling, *Wait, let's try one more time.* Instead she stayed behind the bathroom door while their voices faded and they disappeared from sight.

Then she slumped against the sink, put her face in her hands and cried.

At the end of the hallway Jenine turned left toward her office, and Joseph turned right toward Ricky's room. Pausing, he pulled the giant puppet he'd brought from Italy from its bag, then stood in the hallway untangling strings. He wanted the puppet to be exactly right when he saw Ricky.

Suddenly he froze. What was it? A sound? Instinct? He didn't know. All he knew is that something touched his heart.

"Callie?" he whispered.

He glanced up and down the hallway. Nothing. The

feeling was strong on him, like a wind blowing across a barren dessert.

Following instinct, he backtracked, turned the corner and walked slowly down the hall, swinging his head from right to left, looking, searching. For what? He didn't know.

A sound. A soft click. Alert, Joseph froze. And then he saw it—a door closing.

He strode toward the door, and then stood still. It was the ladies' bathroom. Callie was on the other side of the door. He was certain of it.

"Callie?"

When she heard Joseph call her name she thought she would die. Hand over her heart, she watched the door. What would she do if he came inside?

He knocked, calling to her again, softly. "Callie, are you in there?"

The sound she heard was her heart breaking in two. Slumped against the sink, she closed her eyes while silent tears streamed down her face.

"Callie?" A plea. A sigh. A heart beating in a voice.

Callie put her hand over her mouth to keep from calling to him. There was a small sound, the doorknob turning.

Oh, God, what will I do?

Then suddenly, nothing. No movement. No sound.

Callie wondered if she would faint. Joseph was still on the other side of the door. She felt him as surely as if hot coals were being pressed into her skin.

She tried not to breathe. Sweat beaded her forehead, and her legs began to tremble.

Callie waited. One minute. Two. She lost track of time, and then—footsteps. Distinct as hammers striking metal. Determined. Resolute.

Joseph was going away, but at least, this time, she had been spared another painful goodbye. Callie held her hand over her mouth until the sound of footsteps faded, then she eased out the door and raced toward her car.

Tomorrow she would see Ricky. Tomorrow when Joseph was gone.

Back at her hotel, she finished unpacking. The last thing she took out of her suitcase was Joseph's harmonica. Callie pressed her lips to the cool metal, then set it on the bedside so that when she woke in the middle of the night she could put her hands on it and know that once everything had been real.

The next morning Callie called to be certain that Joseph was not there.

"He told Ricky goodbye yesterday," Jenine told her. "He was on his way to catch a plane."

Back to Italy, Callie thought. A world away.

"Thanks, Jenine. Please tell Ricky I'll see him in a little while."

When Callie opened the door to his room, Ricky was sitting in the middle of the floor talking to a puppet nearly as big as he was. He held one wooden hand and leaned close to the painted wooden face, his expression earnest.

"Joe said to tell you everything. Can I tell you a secret?" Ricky held on to the puppet's long nose and forced the head to nod. "I'm gonna run away and find Callie so we can be a family."

He looked so small and vulnerable sitting there baring his heart to a wooden doll. Silently, Callie made a promise to herself: We're going to be a family, Ricky, no matter what it takes. Just you and me, kid, two against the world.

Then she stuck out her chin, pasted a big grin on her face and braced herself for what she knew was coming.

"Hi, kiddo. Miss me?"

"Callie!" Ricky launched himself at her, grabbed her around the knees and held on tight.

"Hey, if you'll let go, I'll come down there so we can hug each other."

Chin jutted, Ricky tipped back his head so he could see her. "You promise?"

"I promise."

It was an easy promise to keep.

Callie had one more meeting with Jenine before she left Houston for the conference in D.C.

"He's going to try to run away," she told Jenine, "so that he can be with me."

"Don't worry. He's safe here."

"Maybe he's physically safe, but is he emotionally safe? Ricky has formed an emotional attachment to me, Miss Rayborn, and he's determined to be with me, no matter what it takes." She paused for effect. "I'm equally determined to be with him."

Jenine shuffled papers around her desk, then picked up a glass paperweight and toyed with it. Callie plowed into the silence, determined to advance her case.

"I believe I'm the best possible choice you can make for a parent for Ricky, and I'm willing to work with you in any way I can in order to fulfill your requirements. All you have to do it tell me what you need."

Jenine remained quiet. What was she thinking? Had Callie come on too strong? She moderated her tone.

"I really do love him, and he loves me."

Finally Jenine looked at her. "That counts, Dr. Red Cloud."

Chapter Twenty

When Callie got off the plane at Dulles she vowed to put everything behind her except the matter at hand, the International Conference of Virologists. She'd always loved D.C.—the hustle and bustle, the grandeur of the government buildings, the imposing monuments, the art, the deep sense of history.

Being in D.C. always made her think of her own history, of her Apache heritage from her father and her Southern heritage from her mother.

She smiled to think of her mother's people, of their long slow drawls, their love of storytelling, their high-ceilinged houses with the cool porches. Verandas, her Aunt Jessie Queen, her mother's sister, used to remind her. "You're in the Deep South, now, young lady, and don't you forget it."

Callie hadn't thought of Aunt Jessie Queen in years. She'd been dead at least ten. Or had it been longer?

"I wouldn't set foot out the door without a hat," she always said, and her hats were worthy of the society pages: "Jessie Queen Bussard attended a showing at The Gallery wearing one of her famous hats, a confection of pink tulle and satin rosettes with streamers made from real silk Jessie herself brought back from the Orient."

Surrounded by the history of a nation, Callie remembered that bit of family history word for word. Jessie kept all the newspaper clippings about herself in a big pink leather scrapbook with her name embosssed in gold on the cover.

I can give all this to Ricky, she thought. A rich heritage that cuts across ethnic and geographical boundaries.

She would keep his Hispanic heritage alive, as well. Ricky would grow up knowing exactly who he was...and being proud.

The next time I see Jenine Rayborn, I'll tell her all this, Callie thought. It might make a difference.

But for now she was going to focus on the matter at hand. Peg would be joining her tomorrow and they would see the town together in Peg's slapdash, ripsnorting way. Today Callie was going to sightsee her own way, walking, taking her time, making up her own itinerary as she went.

She stayed in front of the Whistler exhibit until closing time, then she took a cab into Georgetown for dinner. By the time she got back to her room she was pleasantly exhausted and asleep by the time her head hit the pillow, which was exactly the way she wanted it.

The next morning, conference madness caught up to her. Hoards of people milled and surged around the conference room, greeting old friends, chatting with colleagues, queuing up at the registration tables.

Callie went to the table labeled *R*. "Red Cloud," she said. "Callie."

The young woman sitting at the table would have looked more at home on a movie set than at a medical conference. Her makeup was perfect, her hair artfully windswept and her body all bones and lean muscle. A Boy Scout in a bra, Peg would have called her.

Callie grinned. Where did they find these young women?

Her name tag said Casandra. She rifled through the files, then pulled out a folder labeled with Callie's name and registration number.

"Here you are, Dr. Red Cloud."

Casandra's enthusiastic bray startled Callie. Where was the hidden mike? Where was the megaphone?

"Thank you."

Callie deliberately spoke quietly, hoping Casandra would take a hint. Her ploy didn't work.

"You're welcome, Dr. Red Cloud. Have a nice day, Dr. Red Cloud."

She might as well have announced Callie over the PA system. Callie tucked her folder into her briefcase, then wove her way through the crowd toward the elevators.

"Callie."

She froze. She didn't have to turn around to know the speaker. She didn't have to see his face. His voice told her everything. It spoke of warm nights in a house trailer in Texas with a small boy cuddled between them. It spoke of deep woods and moonlight and the haunting strains of a harmonica. It spoke of pungent cedar boughs and cool waters and passion so unbridled she lost her breath just thinking about it.

Joseph was at her side now, touching her arm. Just one touch, and Callie trembled inside. She bit the inside of her lower lip. Hard. She had to have pain to divert the tears.

She took a step backward, not enough to look obvious, but enough so that Joseph was no longer touching her. Now she could think. Now she could breathe.

"Joseph…nice to see you."

So cool, so brittle. Was she turning into one of those women she hated? Those artificial creatures with the insincere smiles and the superficial conversations?

"I didn't expect to see you here, Callie."

"I didn't expect you, either."

His eyes searched her face, pierced her soul. But Callie was Apache. She knew how to mask her feelings in the face of the enemy.

The enemy. How had it all happened? How had Joseph gone from colleague to lover to enemy?

The silence stretched for an eternity. Callie gripped her briefcase tighter, trying to anchor herself to the convention hall and the people around her.

But Joseph moved in and bent close. "How have you been, Callie?"

To the casual observer they appeared to be having an ordinary conversation. Only Callie knew the truth: they were in a realm beyond time where eternity could be captured in a single glance, a single word, a single touch.

"How have I been?" she repeated, so softly he had to bend closer. She could see the fine lines spread out from his eyes and the creases of worry on either side of his mouth. "You've lost the right to know, Joseph."

She whirled from him with the intention of striding away, but he caught her arm and fell into step with her.

"So this is how it is between us now," he said. "After all we've been through together."

"Don't you dare bring up the past, Joseph Swift. Don't you dare." She shook him loose once more. "And quit grabbing me."

The wounded look he gave her was genuine. Callie hardened her heart. She had enough on her plate without taking on a single added worry, a single added pain.

"I never meant to hurt you, Callie."

"Who says I'm hurt?"

"You do."

She was saved by the arrival of the elevator. Without a backward glance she hurried inside. Safe.

Just as the doors started sliding shut, Joseph got on and squeezed through so he was standing by her, so close their thighs touched.

Act as if he's not there, Callie told herself. But that was impossible. Every atom in her body was aware of him.

Thank goodness for the crowd. He made no attempt at conversation.

One by one the others left the elevator until they were the only two left, but Joseph never budged from his spot.

Her floor was coming up, and for some perverse reason she didn't want Joseph to know which one was hers.

"What floor?" he asked.

"What's yours?"

Stalemate. They faced off while the elevator door slid open on her floor. She wasn't about to get off, nor was she about to back down. Squared off, they stood there while the doors slid shut once more.

There was only one floor left, and when the doors opened Callie got off. Joseph followed.

"Is your room on this floor?" she said.

"No."

"Where are you going?"

"To your room."

Color slashed her cheeks. Joseph in her bed, covered with nothing but a white sheet. The thrill of it. The joy.

The agony.

"You presume too much," she said.

"To talk. Just to talk." His voice softened. "We never did say goodbye, Callie."

Suddenly all the stiffness went out of her. She didn't want to fight with Joseph. She needed every ounce of her courage in her battle with the state of Texas over custody of Ricky.

"This is not my floor," she said.

"I guessed as much."

"But you followed me anyway."

"I would follow you into hell."

Their eyes met, locked.

"You already did," she whispered.

"Callie…" He reached out to touch her cheek, but she drew back.

"Don't…"

He rammed his hands into his pockets, but not before he clenched them into fists.

"I wish I could change everything that happened," he said.

"What, Joseph? What would you change?" She challenged him with a defiant look. "If you had a second chance would you do a single thing differently?"

She saw his inward struggle, and her heart bled for him. Bled for both of them.

"No," he whispered. "With you I'm caught up in some force beyond my control. I can't look at you without wanting you, without…"

What? Callie wanted to scream, but she knew. Deep down she knew. Behind her the elevator door swung open, and two people got off, a gray-haired man in floral print Bermuda shorts and a woman wearing a wild red wig and bright-yellow pedal pushers. Callie and Joseph stared at each other until the odd couple passed.

"God forbid you should need anybody, Joseph."

She stepped quickly into the elevator just as the doors shut. What was Joseph doing? Standing there watching the floors? Just in case she rode all the way to the bottom, and then back up to her floor.

She felt foolish. It was something a teenager might do. Furious at herself, at him, Callie flung her briefcase into the closet then slumped into a chair. She'd lost her appetite for lunch. She'd lost her appetite for everything except brooding, for that's exactly what she was doing when somebody knocked on the door.

Joseph. Shock waves went through Callie. How did he find her?

The knock came again, and then the sound of a key turning the lock.

"Hey, Callie, are you in there?" The door swung open, and there was Peg. "It's me, your roomie."

Callie could have kissed her. "Welcome," she said.

"My lord, you look like you've seen a ghost." Peg flung her purse in one direction and her shoes in the other. "What's wrong? If it's that old bat in Texas I'll go down there and beat the shucks out of her."

"Why don't you sit down and catch your breath, Peg?"

"If that's your polite way of telling me to mind my own business, you're wasting your breath." Peg surveyed the room. "Umm. Nice. I'm starving. Let's go somewhere and eat a huge high-fat calorie-laden lunch."

And risk running into Joseph? No way.

"I'm a little tired, Peg. You go ahead. I think I'll take a nap."

Peg studied her closely, opened her mouth to comment, then changed her mind and stepped back into her shoes.

"I think I'd better go check the lay of the land," Peg

said casually. Too casually. "I hear Dr. Joseph Swift is going to be here," she added.

"I can never fool you, Peg."

"Why do you even bother trying?"

"That's my stubborn Apache side... Joseph's already here."

"And?"

"For all the good it did we might as well be worlds apart."

"And so you're planning to hole up here for the entire conference so you won't run into him. Is that about right, Callie?"

"You make it sound so cowardly."

"You're no coward, Callie. One of the first things I thought when I met you was, here's a woman with guts, a real grits woman."

"Grits woman?"

Peg grinned. "Girls raised in the South."

"I wasn't raised in the South."

"Yes, but your mother was, and let me tell you, Callie Red Cloud, that kind of courage doesn't wear thin in one generation. Now put on your shoes and let's go to lunch."

Callie not only put on her shoes, but she put on fresh makeup and a fresh dress.

"After lunch, let's go shopping," she told Peg.

"Good lord, is the world about to end? You *never* want to go shopping. What brought that on?"

"Not Joseph, if that's what you're thinking." Callie linked arms with Peg, and the two of them went out the door.

"Did I ever tell you about my Aunt Jessie Queen?"

"No. Jessie *Queen?* She sounds like a hoot."

"She was. And she never went anywhere without a hat.

Aunt Jessie Queen said the whole world looked better from under the brim of a good quality hat.''

Joseph would know that laugh anywhere. He leaned around the potted palm where he'd been sitting with the newspaper, not spying, really, but hoping. Callie and Peg emerged from the elevator, arms linked, laughing.

He started toward them at a fast clip that could only be called a lope. They had their heads close together and they were headed toward the front doors.

The lobby was crowded, and he had to literally push his way through. *Rude.* He knew exactly what people were thinking. He would have thought the same thing himself if some tall rawboned foreigner barreled past him.

"Excuse me," he muttered. "Pardon me."

Thank God Callie was tall. Peg had quickly disappeared in the crowd, but Joseph could still see the top of Callie's head.

Funny how even the top of her head could do crazy things to his heart. He got trapped behind a woman struggling with two stubborn standard poodles on leashes.

Up front he could see the revolving doors moving, see Peg burst into the sunshine with Callie following close behind.

He was losing them. Meanwhile, the poodles wrapped their leashes around the woman, and she was surging this way and that, trying to untangle herself.

The only way around her would be to knock her down. For a crazy moment, Joseph considered doing just that. Fortunately his better judgment won out.

"Can I help you?" he asked her.

"Oh, would you? I can't seem to get Napoleon and Josephine going in the same direction at once."

"Let me take one of those leashes."

The woman thrust the blue one into his hand. "Napoleon," she said. "He's been a very naughty boy today. Mama will have to punish him." The woman lapsed into baby talk, speaking to the dog who showed not the least bit of interest in her. "Mama will have to take away his widdle treat today, yes she will."

Joseph could think of a better punishment. He glanced toward the door. There was no sign of Callie.

"Now you be careful," the woman said. "Napoleon has been known to bite when he's upset."

Great. That's all he needed. A dog bite.

On the other hand, it might be just the thing to restore his sanity. Suppose he had caught up to Callie? What would he have said? She'd made her position perfectly clear, and so had he.

Even if she changed her position, he could not. There was no way he would ever go through the agony of watching the woman he loved expose herself to danger on a daily basis.

Napoleon and his entourage turned out to be a blessing in disguise.

"Good boy," Joseph said, and suddenly the blessing in disguise bared his teeth and growled.

Most people thought Native Americans had a natural affinity for all animals. Joseph was living proof of the fallacy of that kind of thinking.

As he set about separating Napoleon from his owner, he wondered why his blessing in disguise had to come in such a snarling package.

"I look silly."

Callie wore a hat the saleslady had called perky and

Peg had called cute. It was the color of old mushrooms, and that was exactly what it looked like on Callie. Or so she thought. But she kept this opinion to herself. Her mind was on far more important things than the hat.

Joseph. She'd seen him in the lobby, just a glimpse out of the corner of her eye but that was enough to set her mind racing in four different directions.

Why was she so upset? He had made himself perfectly clear on the mountain. So had she, for that matter. She could never love a man who denied his heritage. And yet...

"I think you ought to buy it," Peg said.

"What?"

"The hat. You said you wanted one."

"Maybe not this one." Callie took off the sad-looking mushroom and reached for one with a wide brim that would cover her face if she tilted her head just right. "What about this one?"

"Wow. You look like Greta Garbo, sort of mysterious and sexy and unattainable."

"I agree," the salesclerk said. "It lends you a certain glamorous air."

Callie almost laughed aloud. She'd never been remotely interested in glamour. All her life she'd been called a tomboy, and not without reason. Ellen used to say she spent more time in the barn with the horses than she did in the house with her family. And when she wasn't riding horses, she was picking up stray cats and mangy dogs and birds with broken wings, then taking them to the clinic for Calder to show her how to make them well again.

Still, change was sometimes a good thing.

"I'll take it," she said.

Over lunch Peg kept making Callie adjust the brim until

she was satisfied the hat was at the perfect angle. Callie entered the spirit of the thing, laughing as she tipped it down first so her eyes were barely visible—''It makes you look like a gangster,'' Peg said—then over her right ear at a rakish angle that Peg said made her look like a queen christening a ship.

She settled for the eyes-barely-visible look when all of a sudden she caught a glimpse of a tall dark-haired man, and her breath got caught in her throat.

''What's wrong?'' Peg said.

Callie couldn't speak. All she could do was watch the man at the checkout counter. He turned so his profile was to Callie, and she saw that it wasn't Joseph, after all. She had never expected such acute disappointment, such a sharp sense of loss.

''I thought I saw Joseph, that's all.''

Peg whistled softly. ''You've got it bad, girlfriend.''

''I don't...'' Callie cut off her protest in midsentence. For the past few months she'd done nothing but deny her feelings for Joseph. She, who prided herself on honesty.

''I'm such a fraud, Peg.''

''You are not, and I say that without even knowing what in the devil you're talking about. What are you talking about, Callie?''

''Joseph.''

Peg sighed. ''At last.'' She reached across the table and covered Callie's hand. ''Honey, I knew you'd have to let your feelings out sometime. It's not good to keep them all bottled up the way you have. You should know that.''

''I do. Until now, I didn't even know what I was keeping bottled up. Not really.''

Peg took a bite of her porterhouse steak, waiting. Patience was not her strong suit, and she didn't wait to take a second bite.

"Tell me, for goodness sake. All this uncertainty is bad for my digestion."

"Do you remember when we first went to Houston?"

"Good lord, Callie, are you in one of your musing moods? Darn it, I'm ready for the nitty-gritty."

Callie ignored her friend's impatience. "Do you remember how it was, Peg, with me so bulldog determined to hate Joseph?"

"Yes, but I can't say I remember why."

"Because he denies his Sioux heritage."

"Shoot, who cares? Sorry, Callie. Obviously you do, and I can understand that, I really can."

"Well, I can't. Not anymore."

Callie picked at her salad. Vivid memories of Joseph riding into her camp on Thunderbolt played in her mind, and she smiled.

"Can you believe it?" Callie whispered.

"Believe what? My lord, you're talking in riddles. That's not like you."

"I guess I'm not myself lately. More like somebody waking up from a dream."

"A good one or a bad one?"

"That doesn't matter. What matters is that my stubbornness gave me tunnel vision." Callie could see everything so plainly now. "I was so pigheaded I didn't even see the truth."

Peg shoved her porterhouse steak aside. "For Pete's sake, tell me what you're talking about before I lose interest in dessert, too."

"Don't you see, Peg? It doesn't matter whether Joseph is Sioux or Italian or Chinese. I love him."

Peg smiled. "Strange as this may seem, Callie, you didn't invent that concept. That's what love is, unconditional acceptance."

"I've been such a stubborn fool."

Callie wanted to leap from her seat, race to the hotel and find Joseph. She wanted to blurt out her discovery to him, and...then what? Just because she'd changed her mind, that didn't mean Joseph had changed his.

"Now, what?" Peg said.

"What do you mean?"

"You look like somebody's just turned out your lights." Peg leaned across the table, speaking urgently. "You listen to me, Callie Red Cloud. You're one of the smartest people I know. Maybe too smart for your own good, sometimes. Don't you dare let that mind of yours create obstacles that aren't there. If you love Joseph, then go for it."

"I can't," Callie whispered. "Oh, Peg, don't you see? Joseph made himself very plain from the beginning. After what happened to his wife, he will never get involved with another virologist."

"So what's the problem? You've already quit your job at the center. *Tell* him, Callie."

"You mean try to win him by offering my brand-new not-so-dangerous position up as a bribe? No thanks."

"I see what you mean. I guess you haven't told him about Ricky, either."

"No. And I don't intend to. It's like you said, Peg. Love has to be unconditional."

"Don't worry, Callie. I won't spill the beans."

"Thanks. I didn't think you would."

The waitress came with the dessert menu. "Can we tempt you two with something sweet?"

Peg latched onto her menu. "I can always be tempted with something sweet. How about it, Callie? After all that angst, I think a little self-indulgence is called for."

Callie had no appetite, but why throw a wet blanket on Peg's party?

"I'll have the double chocolate brownie with whipped cream and cherries," she said.

"Way to go, girlfriend!"

Chapter Twenty-One

Joseph walked along the side of the reflecting pool not really knowing where he was headed until he saw the wall. Black granite. Stretching far enough to carry the names of thousands who gave their lives for their country. Cool to the touch, its surface mirroring the gifts of flowers and letters laid at the base and the people who had brought them.

The Vietnam Memorial.

Joseph stood at a distance, watching. People who had been chattering and laughing as they viewed the Lincoln Memorial suddenly became somber. Men took off their caps and bowed their heads. Women held their hands over their hearts, trying to hold back the hurt. Grown children cried.

Such was the power of the wall. Joseph had heard about the effect it had on people, but he'd never expected to be there to see it. Had struggled against being there.

But finally, the struggle was over. The wall loomed before him, beckoning, and he could no longer deny the tug at his heart.

He approached briskly, intending to take a quick walk-through, not even looking at the names. But the closer he came, the more his steps slowed. Names leaped at him from the stone, and a sense of awe stole over him.

He saw himself reflected in the stone, a tall man with cheekbones like knife blades.

You have your father's face.

His mother's voice echoed through the tunnel of mem-ories. Joseph deliberately turned his face away from the wall. He didn't want to have his father's face. He didn't want to have anything that had belonged to Rocky Swift Hawk, including his name.

He spun around, intending to hurry away, when the small piping voice of a child stopped him.

"Was my grandpa a hero?"

The little boy was about the same age as Ricky, a red-haired freckled-face cherub with fat little hands that traced the name carved in stone.

"Yes, Herman, your grandpa was a hero. They're all heroes, the men and women who came back as well as the ones who died."

The young woman was wearing black and carrying a bouquet of yellow roses. At her urging the little boy knelt beside his mother as they placed the roses at the foot of the wall below the long heartbreaking list of names.

Right above the roses Joseph saw it, the name he'd been trying most of his life to avoid. Major Rocky Swift Hawk, USAF. Drawn by a power beyond his control, Jo-seph stood and stared at the name. Images flashed before his eyes—Rocky standing with the other doctors in front of the field hospital, big and bold and full of laughter, daring the fates; Rocky in front of a rice paddy, squatting beside two raggedy little South Vietnamese girls; Rocky lounging in his bunk, dog tags hanging around his bare chest, photos of Sarah and Joseph pinned to the wall behind him.

The album where Sarah kept all the photos had sat on a table in the entry hall until Joseph renounced his name. She'd kept other things there, too—the baseball Rocky used to hit the winning run in a high school game, the dog tags that had been sent to her after his death, a silver-framed photo of Rocky in cap and gown, holding his medical diploma high.

Until Joseph learned the awful truth, he used to stop beside the table every morning on his way to school and touch everything there, everything that had belonged to his father. It was a spiritual ritual, a transfer of power from a great man to the son who would carry on his name.

Joseph sensed movement as the woman and her child stood up.

"Mama, look at that man." The little boy's piping voice cut through Joseph's consciousness.

"Hush, Herman. It's rude to point."

"But Mama…"

"Hush, Herman."

The woman tugged her child away, but their voices drifted back to Joseph on the breeze.

"Mama, why is that man crying?"

"Because he lost a hero, too."

Joseph knelt and pressed his face against the wall.

The seminar, led by the renowned Dr. Claude LeGuen from France's Pasteur Institute, was called "The Houdinis of the Virus World: How They Jump Species."

Claude LeGuen was a mesmerizing speaker, but not

nearly as mesmerizing as the woman who sat at the back of the auditorium on Joseph's left. She was wearing a hat. She and Peg had slid into their seats, flushed and happy, two minutes after Dr. LeGuen took the podium.

"Virus amplification continues to mystify virologists," Dr. LeGuen said.

Callie continued to mystify Joseph. She was different each time he saw her—cool and efficient, warm and accessible, hot and insatiable, polite but distant. She was a multifaceted woman, and every one of them fascinated Joseph.

Callie bent to whisper to Peg, and the outrageously attractive hat she was wearing hid her face. But not the fine black hair. It slid like a bolt of silk over her shoulder, and Joseph felt the quick hot rush of desire.

Up front Dr. LeGuen was talking about pathogenic and nonpathogenic filoviruses. Joseph decided that Callie was pathogenic, capable of causing the disease he now suffered, a disease whose symptoms ranged from insomnia to loss of appetite to outright heartbreak.

What was he going to do about her? About himself? About them?

His mind only halfway devoted to the speaker, Joseph watched Callie out the corner of his eye. She was by turns attentive, restless, animated and pensive. Was she thinking about him?

He prayed she was not, then hoped she was. The conference would last a week, long days and even longer nights of knowing that she was in the same city, the same hotel, the same room.

He had to see her. Alone.

Dr. LeGuen wound up his lecture to resounding applause, and Joseph began to make his way toward Callie, hoping she didn't bolt before he got there. She was only three feet from the door.

Fortunately she got held up in a clot of people. Joseph moved her way as fast as he could, but suddenly a colleague from New York stopped him.

"Joseph! I see you tore yourself away from that beautiful villa."

Sammy Preston clapped Joseph on the shoulder, then blocked his path with 185 pounds of solid muscle. Joseph shifted so he could keep an eye on Callie. Peg was nowhere in sight now, but Callie was still there, head tilted back laughing, surrounded by admirers, every one of them male.

Joseph wanted to punch them all in the face.

"So, how are you, my friend?" Sammy asked.

Murderous. That's how he was. Trapped in the middle of a crowd in a jealous rage because some other man dared look at Callie with a combination of interest and ill-disguised lust.

"I'm great, Sammy, and you?"

Joseph had never known he was such a smooth liar. Of course, before today he'd never had occasion to practice lying.

One of Callie's admirers bent close to whisper something in her ear, and his hand came up to rest on Callie's waist. Joseph balled his hands into fists and rammed them into his pocket.

"Can't complain," Sammy was saying. "Sally and the kids do, though. They say they never see me." He clapped Joseph on the shoulder. "Lucky you're not married."

Across the way, the man's lips were so close to Callie's cheek it looked as if he were kissing her.

"Will you excuse me, Sammy? I have pressing business to take care of."

*   *   *

Callie could have killed Peg for going off and leaving her stranded. She'd seen him coming the minute the seminar was over, a virologist from Kansas who had followed her like a lapdog at every one of these annual seminars.

"Don't look now," she told Peg, "but here comes Mr. Touchy Feely."

"Robert Clayton? I think he's kind of cute." Peg scrambled toward the door. "Ta ta, see you later."

"Peg, come back here."

"I'm doing this for your own good, Callie."

That had been Peg's parting shot, but Callie failed to see the what good it was doing her to be pawed by Robert Clayton. Besides that, he had an irritating way of standing too close and spraying her ear when he talked. And talked. And *talked.*

Everybody else was laughing, so Callie joined in, though she had no idea what the man had said for she'd spotted Joseph heading her way.

"Of course, that wasn't the funniest thing that happened to me in Arizona." Robert squeezed her waist and leaned closer. "I've saved the best for last, Callie."

"Hmm," she said, not the least bit interested in Robert's best.

Nor was anybody else. One by one the rest of the group drifted away. Callie didn't want to be impolite and leave poor Robert in midsentence, but she did wish he would hurry.

Joseph bore down on them. Lightning about to strike.

Robert stood watching her expectantly, and Callie realized he was no longer talking, he was waiting for a comment.

"Hmm," she murmured, because she had no idea what

he'd said. Then because Joseph was looming ever nearer, a cobra coiled for the kill, Callie beamed at Robert.

"Fascinating," she said, and she didn't even hate herself for stooping so low.

"You really think so?"

"Indeed, I do."

Elated, Robert tightened his arm around her and edged closer. He was wearing an aftershave that nauseated Callie.

"You know, Callie, you and I have an awful lot of catching up to do. Why don't we skip out of here and have dinner together?

Suddenly Joseph was there, towering over Robert. "The lady will be occupied this evening." He glowered pointedly at the arm Robert had around Callie. "She's having dinner with me."

"Sorry, old pal. No harm meant." Robert dropped his possessive hold, then scooted toward the door.

The crowd filed out, the auditorium emptied and Callie drowned in Joseph's eyes while conflicting emotions stormed within her—rage, triumph, love.

Rage won. She moved in close, standing toe-to-toe with him.

"How dare you?"

"He was mauling you."

"That's none of your business."

Joseph's eyes were lasers, searching for clues.

"I made it my business when I rode into the White Mountains on your father's horse."

"That's over and done with." Callie snatched up her briefcase and held it in front of herself like a shield. "And so are we."

She tried to push past him to the door, but he caught

her shoulders and held her as easily as if she were a bird in a cage.

"Are we, Callie?"

Her blood was a raging river, its wild song beating in her ears. *No,* she wanted to scream. They would never be through. Neither in this life nor the next. Always, there would be Joseph.

But what did that matter? He would never risk loving her, and suddenly Callie knew that love was all that mattered. Real love. The kind that involves commitment and risk and joy and sorrow and exultation and pain. The kind of love that needs nothing more than a single look, a single touch to forge a bond that nothing can break. The kind of love her parents had.

When she finally spoke, her voice was barely above a whisper, and certainly without conviction. But Callie was beyond caring. All she wanted to do was get through the conference in one piece, then go home and lick her wounds and start all over again.

"Yes. We're finished." Amazing that she could tell an outright lie without even blinking.

"You would deny everything we were, everything we had?"

The great Dr. Swift, famous for keeping his feelings under wraps, let his mask slip. Lord, why did he have to look like a wounded warrior? Why did he have to be so compelling?

Callie's only defense was to go on the warpath.

"What were we, Joseph? What did we have? A few chance encounters, a few laughs?" She forced a brittle laugh. "It happens every day. Men and women are like trains—they meet, link up for a while then go off on separate tracks."

She wanted to have the last word, then stalk toward the door, but Joseph's eyes pinned her to the spot.

"Bravo, Callie. That's a convincing speech." A muscle ticked in his jaw and his fingers bit into her upper arms. "I don't buy it, Callie...any of it."

"It doesn't matter whether you believe it or not. *I* believe it, Joseph, and that's all that counts."

She tipped her chin back and glared at him, but it didn't work. Nothing worked. He was undressing her with his eyes, kissing her with his eyes, making love to her with his deep, dark eyes.

Tangled in a web of memories, she melted, and so did he. His grip loosened, softened, and he caressed her shoulders. She felt herself going slack, felt her knees giving way, felt herself leaning toward him.

"No," she whispered.

"Yes," he said. "A part of you belongs to me, Callie. A part of you will always belong to me."

Wanting and needing and loving rushed through her. If he had said the word, Callie would have spread herself on the floor of the auditorium and given herself to this beloved warrior, this magnificent Sioux. In a public place. Without shame. Without regret.

He saw it all in her face. She could tell by the way his eyes darkened.

Please. Was it a word, a thought, a sigh? Callie didn't know. All she knew was that Joseph had suddenly turned gallant and tender.

"I'm sorry, Callie. My only excuse is that I lose all perspective around you."

He rammed his hands into his pockets, but neither of them could move. Somewhere in the distance a door opened, and there was the sound of a vacuum cleaner. Still, their eyes held each other captive.

Finally Joseph broke the silence.

"Do you have plans for dinner?" If he had been arrogant or presumptuous or the least bit possessive, Callie would have said yes. But Joseph's invitation was simple, straightforward, and friendly, one colleague to another. Almost.

"No," she said.

"Would you join me? Please?"

It was the *please* that did it for Callie.

"Yes, I'll have dinner with you."

"Is seven all right with you?"

"Fine. I'll meet you in the lobby."

When Callie got back to her room, Peg was practically bouncing off the walls with curiosity and excitement.

"What happened?" she said. "Tell me now and don't leave out a thing."

"I'm having dinner with Joseph tonight."

Peg did a jig around the room. "I knew it! There's not a man born who won't rise to the challenge when he sees somebody else horning in on his territory."

"I'm not territory, and I was merely talking to Touchy Feely. Not using him. I wouldn't stoop so low."

"Yeah, but it worked, didn't it?"

Wicked glee beats righteous anger every time. Callie burst into laughter.

"Lord, Peg, what am I going to do with you? You're corrupting me."

"Good." Peg plopped onto the bed and patted the mattress. "Sit down now, and tell me what you're wearing tonight. And don't you dare say that somber black thing I saw hanging in the closet."

"That's the one."

"It most certainly is not. If you're going to fish you need to use the right bait."

"I have a hard time thinking of myself as bait, but I'll humor you. What do you suggest?"

"There is the most incredible dress in the shop downstairs." Peg bounced off the bed and grabbed her purse. "Come on, I'll show you. And on the way down you can tell me word for word everything that was said."

"I don't need a new dress," Callie said, but she got her purse anyway. After all, what would it hurt to look her best?

Callie wore red. She looked stunning, elegant, and so sexy that Joseph wanted to kill every man who looked at her. The dress was tantalizing and demure at the same time, caught high around her throat with a band of rhinestones in the front and plunging all the way to her waist in the back. The fabric was the soft clingy type that molded her body, and through the thigh-high slit he caught just a glimpse of leg.

To add to the allure, Callie had swept her hair up then left a few tendrils trailing down her long, slender neck.

Joseph took it all in with one glance. And then to be sure he hadn't missed a thing, he took another long look.

Dinner was going to be the most dangerous thing he'd done in years.

Chapter Twenty-Two

"It's a beautiful night for walking," she said.

"Only if we want to be mugged."

Joseph hailed a cab, then sat close enough to smell her perfume but not close enough to get her dander up. Callie, he'd discovered, had a temper. And he liked it.

He liked everything about her, including the way she ate. He'd seen her eat before, of course, but only fish, pork and beans out of the can and those rushed meals in the midst of the outbreak. He'd never seen her enjoy a leisurely meal.

It was one of the ways a man could learn about a woman.

"Hmm. Marvelous."

She closed her eyes and moaned deliciously over the macadamia nut soup. Joseph died a little inside.

It was a sound he'd heard before. In the White Mountains. Beside the waterfall.

The shrimp scampi with dill cream sauce caused her to roll her shoulders in ecstacy, all the while making little appreciative sounds that drove him wild.

"I love watching you eat," he said.

She laughed, then dug into her black goma asparagus. He was fascinated.

"I would never have guessed," he said. "You're so slender."

"I work it off." Her eyes danced with devilment. "In a variety of ways."

He bit down on a moan. God, how was he ever going to be able to say goodbye to this woman again?

"Their dessert menu is one of the best in town," he said. "I can't decide between the coconut yum yum and the macadamia nut banana cake."

"Neither can I." She set her dessert menu aside and looked him straight in the eye. "I think I'll have both."

Joseph roared. This is how it should be with a man and a woman, he thought. Easy camaraderie. Fun. And always the underlying sexuality.

"It's obvious you love eating. Do you love cooking, Callie?"

"Yes. When I have time. I'm a gourmet cook."

"Then you would love Italy. Have you ever been there?"

"No. Spain, Portugal, France, but not Italy. Tell me about it."

"You'd love it for the food alone."

It was her turn to laugh. "Are you implying that I have a healthy appetite?"

"I can testify to the fact." He captured her with a look. "You have a healthy appetite for all things."

They were wading in dangerous waters. It wouldn't be fair to take her there. Not again. Bruised hearts were too easily broken, and the last thing he wanted to do was break Callie's heart.

After he left the mountain he'd never expected to see her again, and yet here she was, sitting across the table from him in Washington D.C. Joseph had been given a second chance, and he knew they were rare.

This time, he intended to get it right. Callie was one in a million, a warm and beautiful woman, a brilliant virologist who deserved more than a few days in a mountainside camp with a man who could never pledge his love "till death do us part."

Death was always so close. One prick of a needle, one slip of a mask, one mistake.

Joseph would make no mistakes this time. He had a few days to treat Callie the way she deserved to be treated, the way he should have treated her from the beginning: as a valued colleague and good friend.

"One of my favorite spots is a little town nestled at the foot of the Subasio Mountains," he said. "Assisi."

"The home of Saint Francis."

"Exactly. In the evening when the bells ring and the cypress trees dance and the white doves lift off on wings that glow in the sunset, you can feel his spirit."

Enraptured, Callie leaned across the table. "That's poetry, Joseph."

"You love poetry, don't you, Callie?"

"Yes. That's how my father courted my mother."

Her hand lay on the white linen cloth, golden-skinned and slender. Joseph covered it with his own.

"That's how you deserve to be courted."

He felt the tremor that ran through her. He wanted to lift her hand to his lips, to feel the soft touch of her skin, to taste the sweetness he knew so well.

But he had no right. Too much stood between them. A

dangerous profession. A struggle over identity. And soon, an entire ocean.

No, he had no right.

"Someday, Callie, someone will court you that way."

Silently she withdrew her hand, but her face was composed, giving away nothing.

"It's getting late," she said.

"Yes. I'll call for a cab."

On that long cab ride back to the hotel, the ocean already flowed between them. It wasn't that they didn't talk. That would have been too obvious. It was what they talked about: how the White House looked at night, the traffic in D.C., the conference schedule.

Polite small talk.

Their hotel loomed. In a few minutes Callie would go to her room and he would go to his. Alone.

He said goodbye to her in the lobby. It would be easier, he'd decided. Easier to watch her walk away into a crowd than to watch her walk into her bedroom and lock him out.

"Thank you for dinner, Joseph."

"It was my pleasure, Callie."

The lobby was still crowded. Snatches of conversation drifted around them. Virologists loved nothing better than to stand around talking about their work. Ordinarily Joseph would be an avid participant, but not tonight.

Tonight there was nothing except Callie in red, Callie with the startling blue eyes and the silky hair, Callie with the mind and body that drove him wild. He longed to touch her, to taste her, to take her into his arms and never let her go.

She was close...yet so very far away.

He trembled with the effort to keep his distance. "Good night, Callie."

"Night, Joseph."

Hesitant, she stood in front of him a moment longer. All he had to do was reach out to her. Conscience warred with desire.

Callie turned swiftly, then three feet away she looked over her shoulder and smiled. "Sweet dreams." She merely mouthed the words, but they were bells ringing through his mind.

He watched until she was in the elevator, then he spun on his heel and headed back out the door. He was in a murderous mood. He needed air.

The elevator was empty. Callie held herself together until the doors closed, then she leaned her face against the wall and cried. She had the elevator all to herself until she reached her floor. There was a light showing under the door.

"Good grief, what happened to you?"

Peg tossed her book on the table and caught hold of Callie's arms. For once Callie didn't try to be brave in the face of adversity.

"I can't do this anymore." Her shoulders shook as she let the sobs rip.

Peg pulled Callie into her arms. "That's right, you let it all out. Cry to your heart's content. That's the way."

Callie accepted the comfort and thanked God for the friendship. Another woman always understood tears.

She cried until there were no more tears, then she went into the bathroom and washed her face. When she came out Peg was perched on the edge of the bed.

"Sit down. If you want to talk about it, I'll listen. If you don't want to talk, I'll shut up and offer a fairly substantial shoulder."

"I think I need to talk this through, but let me get this dress off first. I look ridiculous."

"You look gorgeous."

"Thank you, but that's beside the point. I've never tried to be anybody but myself, and I'm not planning to start now." She stepped out of the dress and tossed it to Peg. "If you can wear it, it's yours."

"Are you kidding? You've got about eight feet of legs and no hips." Peg folded the dress and put it into Callie's suitcase. "Someday you'll want to wear it again."

"And this hat." Callie snatched it out of the closet and flung it onto the bed. "What on earth was I thinking of?"

"Aunt Jessie Queen." Peg put the hat on and looked at herself in the mirror. "My lord, I look like an elf under a toadstool. Mike would die laughing." She packed the hat into Callie's suitcase. "By the way, did you notice that you're not crying anymore?"

"If I start again, I might never stop."

Callie slid into her robe, then wrapped her arms around herself. Loss stabbed her like knives, and she wondered if she would ever be free of the pain.

"Tonight I realized something, Peg. I'm not a brittle sophisticated woman who can go from loving a man one minute to being his best buddy the next. I'm not the kind of woman who can sit across from the man I want above all things on this earth and pretend that nothing is wrong."

"Bravo. Tell Joseph."

"You mean try to shock him into making the same confessions? No, thank you. He's made his position perfectly clear. I have no intention of playing the role of beggar."

"No one would dare think of you that way, Callie. You're the strongest woman I know."

Callie walked to the window and gazed out into the night. It had started to rain. Streetlights cut a bright path in the darkness, and in one small arc stood a tall man, his collar pulled high, his shoulders hunched forward as if the burden on them was too heavy to bear.

Joseph.

Callie squinted into the darkness trying to pick out his features. He was too far away. She couldn't tell a thing about him except that he was tall.

She had to stop doing that. She couldn't go through the rest of her life losing her breath at the sight of every tall man she encountered. She couldn't spend the rest of her days scanning crowds for a glimpse of hair as black as a raven's wing and cheekbones like knife blades.

Closing her eyes, she rested her forehead on the windowpane.

"I'm so tired of being strong and brave," she whispered.

Peg slid her arm around Callie's shoulders and stood beside her, silent.

Sometimes, deliverance came in the smallest gestures imaginable.

Callie was not at the morning session. Joseph searched the auditorium for her. He spotted Peg up front with two virologists from California, but Callie was nowhere in sight.

After the lecture he hurried to the bank of phones in the hallway and had the desk clerk call her room. If she was there, she wasn't answering the phone.

He prowled the lobby, the gift shops, the coffee shops looking for her. There was no sign of her. He even started asking have-you-seen-this-woman questions that made people give him funny sidelong glances, as if he might be a prime candidate for the little men in white coats.

He did a block by block search around the hotel, missing his lunch completely. How could he eat when his heart was around his ankles? By the time he got back to the hotel, the afternoon session was in full swing. He skipped it. An unprecedented thing for him.

He tried her room once more. No answer. Agony ripped him apart. To be in the same hotel and not see her was unbearable. He had only a few days left in D.C. and every moment with Callie was precious.

He slipped in the door of the conference room, but he didn't have the lecture on his mind. He was looking for Peg. If anybody knew where Callie was, it was her friend.

He spotted her near the back, on the opposite side of the auditorium. Up front Dr. Karla Langerfeld was talking about "Regulation of a Runaway Replicator," but Joseph listened with only half his mind. The other half was occupied with watching Peg to be certain he got out the door before she did.

After the lecture, he caught up with her in the hallway in front of the bank of elevators.

"Peg, I need to talk to you."

"Sure." She came to him, smiling. "Shoot."

"Not here. How about a cup of coffee?"

"Great." She linked her arm through his. "You're the first handsome man who's asked me to coffee since I left Mike in Atlanta. How have you been, pal?"

"Busy. I'm headed to the Ivory Coast after the conference to join a research team. How about you?"

They slid into a back booth at the coffee shop downstairs.

"In about eight months, I'm headed to the maternity ward. I'm pregnant, and you're the first to know." Peg picked up the dessert menu. "Buy me a double chocolate sundae with whipped cream and nuts and lots of cherries,

Joseph, and I'll kill you if you tell Callie or Mike before I do. Lord, I don't know what got into me.''

"I do.'' Joseph grinned.

"Where were you hiding that wicked sense of humor while we were in Texas?''

"I never mix work with pleasure.''

"Maybe you should.''

Maybe she was right, he thought. Since Maria's death he'd taken himself entirely too seriously. The waitress came, and he ordered black coffee for himself and the sinfully rich concoction for Peg. Then he got straight to the point.

"Where's Callie?'' He saw Peg's struggle with herself. "I'm not asking for secrets, Peg, nor even for particulars. I respect Callie's privacy.''

"Lord, you don't know how that relieves my mind. I'd hate to lie to a man who just bought me a thousand calories of sin.''

"Is she still in D.C.''

"Yes, she's still here. And that's all I'm telling you.''

"That's all I want to know. Will you take her a message for me?''

"You know I will. I love being in the middle of things.''

Joseph scrawled his message on the napkin, then handed it to Peg.

"Thanks, Peg. If there's anything I can ever do for you, let me know.''

Peg was quiet a long time, then she took both his hands and squeezed.

"Don't break her heart, Joseph.''

Chapter Twenty-Three

Callie spent the day in the botanical gardens. In D.C. that was as close as she could get to nature. Among the ferns and hosta lilies she found a sense of peace that evaded her in the hotel.

She didn't request a guided tour. Callie was not searching for knowledge: she was searching for the truth within herself. She stayed until the gardens closed, and then she took a taxi back to the hotel.

Peg greeted her with soft hugs and cluckings of concern.

"I'm going to be fine," Callie said.

"You don't know what a relief that is to me. I worried about you today…and that's not good for a woman in my condition."

"What condition?"

"I'm going to have a baby."

The news hit Callie like a blow to the solar plexus, and it took her a while to adjust.

"I didn't mean to tell you, but…oh, I don't know. I got one of those little kits and didn't have the courage to use it till last night, and I haven't even told Mike yet because I want to tell him face-to-face, but…gosh, news like that is too good to keep, don't you think?"

"I do," Callie said. "I've been selfish. Tonight we celebrate, and we're going to talk about nothing but you."

Callie meant that, too.

"Before you make any rash promises, I have something for you. From Joseph."

Callie unfolded the napkin. Written in bold strokes, the message leaped out at her: Callie, I'm sorry. I want to tell you in person. Call me. Please. Joseph, Room 615.

She folded the note and tucked it into her pocket. "Let's go, Peg." She was determined to keep her word to Peg if it killed her.

But that didn't keep her from scanning every crowd for a glimpse of a tall Sioux warrior who held her heart captive.

Joseph waited in his room all evening, but Callie didn't call. He called downstairs and ordered room service, not because he was hungry but to be certain his phone was working.

The food sat untouched, while he read the latest publication from the National Institute of Virology. Before he went into the bathroom, he dragged the telephone as far as the cord would reach, then took a bath rather than a shower so he could hear the phone. If Callie called he didn't want to trust her message to the hotel staff.

At midnight he decided she wasn't going to call. But he put the phone right beside his pillow. Just in case.

* * *

For the next three days, Callie practiced the art of evasion. She waited until the very last minute to enter the lecture halls, stood at the back scanning the crowd until she spotted Joseph, then took at seat on the opposite side of the auditorium, close to the door.

But his note burned in Callie's mind. Daily she argued with herself. She would see him, it was the least she could do, all he wanted was to apologize, after all. What harm could come of it? Her mind whirled with controversy.

In the end it was the harmonica that made up her mind.

For all practical purposes the conference was over. Virologists checked out of the hotel in droves, crowding the lobby with their suitcases and armloads of books.

Callie went downstairs to see Peg off.

"Are you sure you don't want me to go to the airport with you, Peg?"

"Absolutely not. Get some rest, Callie. You've worn yourself out avoiding Joseph."

"Was I that obvious?"

"It couldn't have been plainer if you had written it on a billboard."

Good, Callie thought.

Then she went back to her room and crashed. Something startled her awake—a sound, a dream, a teardrop. Her face was wet. She'd been crying in her sleep.

It was dark outside, and rain slashed the window. Her bedside clock said ten. Stumbling into the bathroom to splash water on her face, Callie caught a glimpse of herself in the mirror. She looked haunted.

"The harmonica," she whispered.

That's what had startled her awake. She still had Joseph's harmonica.

Her heart racing, she went back into the bedroom, picked up the phone and dialed.

Be there, she silently pleaded. Please be there.

The phone rang four times. Five. Six. What if he had already checked out? What if he had gone back to Italy?

Callie started to cradle the receiver when she heard his voice.

"Hello." For a moment she couldn't speak. "Hello. Is anyone there?"

"Joseph."

"Callie? Is that you?"

Her hand tightened on the receiver. "I need to see you."

"I'll come right up," he said.

Callie panicked. If she let him into her bedroom, she would never have the heart to ask him to leave. Control would be in his hands.

"No, I'll come there."

Silence. What was he thinking? What did it matter? She would be in charge. She would enter, state her piece, and leave. Just that simple.

"I'll be waiting," he said.

Stunned, Joseph replaced the receiver. Callie had avoided him for days, and now she was coming to his room. It was beyond comprehension.

But then, Callie was not the kind of woman you could predict. That was part of the fascination.

Joseph shoved the suitcase he'd been packing into the closet and shut the door. Tidying up. As if that mattered. He checked the bathroom to be sure he hadn't left wet towels on the floor. It was a totally useless errand. Joseph never left wet towels on the floor. He never even left a dirty coffee cup in the sink.

He ran a comb through his hair, and was sitting at the window when she knocked. He straightened a pillow on the way to the door. And there she was, as if he'd dreamed her, backlit by the hall lights, hair shining, eyes glowing. He didn't trust himself to speak. All he could do was stare at her like a shipwrecked seaman who had finally caught a glimpse of the shore.

"May I come in?"

He noticed her smile didn't touch her eyes, and guilt smote him. Was he the cause?

He held the door open, and she stepped into his room. Suddenly the bed loomed, took on enormous significance, and it struck Joseph that he had never made love to Callie in a real bed. They had loved on blankets and cedar boughs and seashores and even in the depths of the lake, but never on a bed with her hair fanned out on the pillow and her skin glowing golden against the white sheets.

As if she knew what he was thinking, her gaze traveled to the bed, then back to him. Joseph rammed his hands into his pockets to keep from touching her.

He had made that mistake once. He would never do it again. His obsession had hurt Callie, and Joseph had no intention of hurting this woman again. Ever.

"Joseph, I don't want you to get the wrong idea about my coming here."

"You know me better than that. I would never presume anything with you, Callie. Won't you sit down?"

So polite. As if she were a stranger. As if he had never shared an intimate moment with her. As if he had never known her deepest mysteries.

Callie perched on the edge of a chair, her chin thrust forward, her back upright, her expression determined. Joseph wanted to take her in his arms and caress that stiff back until she relaxed. He wanted to smooth her silky hair until she melted against him, boneless and yielding.

But he had no right.

"You're leaving tomorrow?" she asked.

"Yes. And you?"

"I'm leaving on an early morning flight."

It was small talk fraught with significance. What they were saying to each other was this: I'll go my way and you go yours.

Joseph discovered he had deep reservoirs of pain that had never been tapped. Loss stormed him, and he had to use Herculean effort to remain in his chair, to keep from leaping across the table, grabbing Callie and yelling, "I don't care about any of it, I don't care about your job, I don't care about heritage, I don't care as long as I can have you."

He was selfish. Thinking only of himself, his needs, his desires. It surprised Joseph to think of himself that way.

Tonight, he had been given a chance to redeem himself.

"Callie, I'm so glad you came. After the past few days I was afraid you wouldn't respond to my note."

"It wasn't the note that brought me here. It was this...."

She reached into her pocket and pulled out his harmonica. Her fingers closed around it briefly, then she laid it on the table between them.

Memories swarmed through Joseph: the campfire, the full moon, the night breezes, and the two of them warding off the chill by holding each other close.

Callie's eyes were suspiciously bright. Was she thinking the same thing?

"It belongs to you," she said.

He made no move toward the harmonica. As vividly as if it were yesterday he remembered seeing her emerge from her tent, discover the harmonica then lift it to her lips. All these lonely weeks he had enjoyed thinking of her that way, putting her lips where his had been, perhaps caressing the silver, thinking of him, missing him, wanting him.

"Keep it," he said.

"No."

He had never known a woman who could make getting up from a chair an act of grand defiance. Like some angry goddess arising from Mount Olympus, Callie towered over him, her eyes shooting sparks.

"Isn't that exactly like you, Joseph? Arrogant. Presumptuous. Self-important."

God, she was glorious when she was mad. Joseph was so busy admiring her, he had a hard time concentrating on what she was saying. She came around the table, stalking him.

"What do you think I am, Joseph Swift? Some starstruck little teenager who wants a bauble that belongs to the great doctor from Italy? Somebody who's going to moon over you? Do you think I'm going hold on to your harmonica and weep?"

He stood so fast his chair toppled over. In one swift move he captured Callie's lips. The contact sent shock waves through him, and he had a hard time sticking to his purpose. He wanted to shock Callie into silence, not set his own blood racing. He wanted to regain his control, not lose it.

And yet...

Moaning, Callie parted her lips to give him access. Without thought, without design, he plunged his tongue into the soft inner recesses, tasting once again that hot honeyed sweetness that drove him mad.

She moved in his arms so that their bodies were fitted perfectly together, and Joseph clung to his sanity by a thread. Just a while longer. Just one more taste. And then he would let her go. Then he would be in control.

She bloomed in his arms. He could feel her soft yielding, feel the melting of her body, the bending of her will.

It would be so easy to take her. A few steps and they would be on the bed. A flick of the wrist and her clothes would be on the floor.

Need was a tiger, clawing his back, snarling deep in his throat. He wanted to grind himself into her, to feel the sweet relief as her hot flesh closed around him.

Her arms stole around his neck, and Joseph trembled on the brink of disaster. He was torn in two. His heart yearned for completion while his mind screamed danger.

A soft whimpering sound of sheer need escaped Callie, but Joseph took no pleasure from the sound. He wouldn't allow himself that. Callie was vulnerable. Only a cad would take advantage of her.

Every nerve in his body screaming, Joseph pulled back. Callie raked her hair back, her hands shaking. But she didn't step back. Not his Callie. Eyes blazing, she looked up at him.

"Are you quite finished, or is there something else you want from me?" Deliberately she moved in on him, so close he could see the flecks of gold in the centers of her sky-blue eyes. "Before I go, perhaps you'd like another taste of the mirror dance? Or is it the medicine wheel you have in mind?"

"I didn't know you had claws, Callie."

"All cats have them. Didn't you know?"

In one smooth featherlight sensual movement, she raked her fingernails down the side of his face.

"There are lots of things you don't know about me, Joseph Swift...things you will never find out."

He caught her wrist and looked deep into her eyes, trying to read her. But she had shut herself off from him.

No, he would never find out. The knowledge saddened him beyond imagining.

"Callie, don't do this."

She tried to jerk away from him, but he held her fast.

"You're the one who started it. I just came here to talk."

Something wild and perverse broke lose in him. Something savage. Something that put polite reserve to rout.

"Is that why you kissed me back?"

She wrenched herself free. "Go back to Italy, Joseph. Go back and take your damned harmonica with you."

She whirled around and was halfway to the door before his brain could function.

"Callie, wait…"

For a fraction of a second he thought she would keep on going, but she turned around and the look on her face drove a stake through his heart.

"Don't you ever kiss me again. Don't you ever touch me again—" her voice dropped to a whisper "—unless you mean it."

She glided through the door quickly, a ghost, a wraith, a phantom, already a part of his past.

He couldn't let her go this way. Not with anger and tears. He'd never even said he was sorry.

He raced to the door and caught the handle…then leaned his head against the door and shut his eyes.

It was better this way, better for her to hate him than to spend one moment in the lonely agony of defeat.

"Goodbye, my love," he whispered.

Chapter Twenty-Four

If it hadn't been for airport security, Joseph would be on his way back to Italy. They'd pulled him aside to search his bag.

"What's wrong?" he asked.

"Something that looks like a hammer."

They pawed through his belongings until they found what they sought.

"What is it?" the security guard asked him.

After Joseph left the Black Hills he had put the pipe out of his mind, but there it was in the hands of a stranger, the red clay pipe with its carvings and its adornment of eagle feathers.

The sacred pipe. His destiny.

"It's just a souvenir I picked up on my travels to South Dakota," Joseph said, knowing a simple explanation would be easier to understand.

Satisfied, the guard searched through the rest of the bag's contents.

"All set, sir," he said.

"Thanks." Joseph picked up his bag and headed back through the security gates.

"Hey, you're going the wrong way," the guard called after him.

"No, I'm finally going the right way."

The house nestled in a garden around the bend from the clinic. Mountains rose behind it and a stream meandered through the east side of the gardens, spanned by a small arching bridge Callie's grandfather had built.

He had built the house, as well, and after he died her grandmother stayed on in spite of failing health, bound by her deep love of the garden. She'd called her place Eden, and it had stood empty since her death six years earlier.

Now it was Callie's house.

Sitting on a curving wooden bench in the garden, she tested the words aloud, and the sound of them brought joy to her. Her house rang with laughter and blazed with lights, but she stayed in the garden awhile longer. A moonvine had opened, its blossoms shining stark white under the stars, scattering their fragrance throughout the garden.

She heard the back door open and shut.

"Callie." It was her brother calling to her from the back porch. "Everything all right out here?"

"I'm fine, Eric."

The moonlight silhouetted him, a tall man with high cheekbones and a handsome nose. He came toward her slowly. Eric did everything with an economy of movement and a tranquility that Callie envied.

In time, maybe she would acquire his great sense of peace.

He propped one foot on the wooden bench. ''Mom's worried about you.''

''I know. It's my housewarming party, and I'm selfish to linger in the garden.''

''Call it self-preservation.''

Callie stood and linked arms with her brother. ''Brenda's a lucky woman.''

''We're both lucky.'' He squeezed her hand. ''Someday you will be, too. If that man had a brain in his head.''

''Shhh. He's brilliant.''

''Maybe that's his problem. He's too cerebral. Love defies logic.''

Callie's laughter was fond. ''I don't think that's a new concept, Eric.''

''I should have told that to Brenda. She thinks everything I say is original and brilliant.''

''Smart woman.''

Callie could see her sister-in-law through the French doors, her belly big with child. Envy stabbed her. Always tuned in to her moods, Eric squeezed her hand.

''It's going to be all right, Sis. When Jenine Rayborn sees this place and this family, she's going to fall all over herself trying to rush that adoption through.

Callie was too much a realist to think that would happen, especially in the face of Jenine's early opposition.

''You're not buying it, are you?''

''You know me too well, Eric.''

Calder Red Cloud appeared on the back porch, his mane of white hair gleaming in the moonlight. Callie thought he looked like a fine old mountain lion, poised and regal in spite of the slight droop to his shoulders.

She and Eric paused a moment, awestruck by their father.

"Callie? Eric? Are you out here?"

"Here we are." Eric moved them into a path of moonlight so Calder could see.

"Good. I think I'll join you. There's too much racket inside."

He moved slower than he used to, but he was still majestic. Callie and Eric waited for him beside a weeping Japanese cherry tree their grandmother had ordered from a nursery in South Carolina.

"How can Jenine doubt that this is the best place for Ricky when she meets him?" Eric nodded toward their father.

Callie couldn't help but think it was so. When their father came abreast, she took his arm on one side and Eric, the other.

Calder lifted his face toward the sky. "Ahhh, that's better. Peace."

"Are you all right, Dad?"

Calder snorted. "Fit as a fiddle. You're practicing medicine on the wrong person, Daughter. Save your skills for the clinic."

"I have plenty left over for you."

"That's what I'm afraid of." He winked at his son. "I don't know why I wanted her to come back home. She's going to make my life pure hell."

"I intend to."

Suddenly Callie blossomed, like a puny philodendron that had been given a large dose of root fertilizer. She loved this friendly sparring with her family.

It was good to be home.

Calder bent down, grasped a handful of earth and held

it to his nose. "Ahhh," he said. Then he straightened up slowly and pressed the dirt into Callie's hand.

"The dust of our ancestors is here, Callie. The ashes of their council fires are cold and white, and smoke curls no more from their lodges, but their spirit remains. A strong and powerful totem. We are not birds with a broken wing—we are The People, proud and brave."

When her father spoke of the old ways he was transformed, no longer a modern man who had studied medicine at Harvard, but an ancient Apache shaman, with a soul full of poetry and a mind full of healing secrets revealed to him through the Great Spirit.

Callie loved it when her father was like this. Rapt, she and Eric listened.

"My bones are growing weary, and soon I'll rest with our ancestors, but the two of you will carry on. You will tell the stories to your children and grandchildren, and they will teach the old ways to their children. The People will live forever.

He took their hands and joined them over his heart, then he kissed Callie's cheek.

"That's why you're home, Daughter." Calder brushed the tears from her cheek. "Come now. Let's go back inside. Your mother is waiting for us."

Joseph's spirit quest to the sacred land of the Sioux was a solitary one, made on horseback as his ancestors had done in the days of old. As he approached his destination it was easy to see why the Sioux considered the Black Hills sacred. Tall needles of rock touched the sky, warm springs flowed through the Hills, and crystal beckoned from hidden caves.

The father of Crazy Horse had journeyed to one of the peaks and received supernatural healing powers from a spirit in the form of a bear. The peak was named Bear Butte in honor of the great shaman.

Another of the majestic rock formations, Harney Peak, had been off-limits to the Sioux because the Thunderbird often visited there, hurling thunderbolts, shouting with tongues of lightning and whipping up violent winds.

Joseph's mother had told him all the legends, and when he was young he had believed in the mystery and the power of the spirit quests. Somewhere along the way he'd lost that belief.

He reined his horse to a standstill. As far as he could tell, he was alone in the sacred hills. The setting sun tipped the peaks with red gold, then plunged behind the Hill of Thunder where the white giant who once spewed smoke into the sky lay sleeping. The sky caught fire, and it glowed with colors so brilliant they hurt the eye. Then slowly the embers died down, and dusk settled over the land.

Cocooned in darkness, Joseph sat on his horse listening to the silence. According to legend, the rocks turned into spirits at night that roamed the land and sang strange, haunting songs. And sometimes the white giant who lay beneath the Hill of Thunder moaned because of the rocks pressing down on his chest.

Unconsciously, Joseph was listening for rocks that sang and hills that moaned. Instead he heard a silence so complete he might have vanished off the face of the earth.

Because of its connection to the ancient medicine men, Joseph placed his bedroll at the foot of Bear Butte near the mouth of a crystal cave. Then he slept his first dreamless night in years.

Jenine Rayborn came to the clinic on one of the busiest days of the year.

There was a mild epidemic of chicken pox at the schools, and twenty children sat in a squirming, itching row along the wall of the clinic with twenty concerned parents trying to keep order. In addition, Glenn Little Bear's barn had collapsed during a barn raising, and a dozen men with assorted broken bones sat complaining in rocking chairs and on the steps of the front porch.

Callie wanted to scream. Instead she ushered Jenine into her small office at the back of the clinic and offered her coffee.

"I'm afraid I don't have time to show you around. As you can see, the clinic is full."

"Yes, so I see. The clinic keeps you awfully busy, doesn't it?"

"Generally, no. Yesterday we had only five people. This is an unusual day." Callie told her about the chicken pox and the collapsed barn.

"Hmm, I see."

No, you don't, Callie wanted to say, but she bit her lip and kept her silence. Ricky's future depended on her performance in front this woman. Ranting and raving would neither help him nor advance Callie's case.

Jenine took in the office while she sipped her coffee. Suddenly Callie saw the clinic through her eyes, a log cabin that looked like it might have grown out of the mountains, modest in size, not very impressive if you compared it to the architectural wonders most doctors preferred.

"My father built this clinic." Callie spoke with pride. "He wanted the kind of place where people would feel comfortable to come for healing."

Jenine pursed her lips. "I see."

She didn't see at all. Callie's spirits fell.

"Daughter, your patients are waiting."

Suddenly her father was there, his slightly bent frame filling the doorway, his powerful voice filling the room.

"And you must be Miss Rayborn."

Calder bent over her hand in a courtly gesture that would sway stone. For the first time in days, Callie felt hope.

"Miss Rayborn, this is my father, Calder Red Cloud."

"Why don't I show Miss Rayborn around until you're free, Callie?"

He offered his arm, and when she left the room, Jenine was smiling. Callie took that as a good sign.

Her father's voice drifted back to her.

"Before I built this clinic some of my people were still depending on shamans who smeared them with grease and ashes."

Callie stuck her head around the door frame and watched them disappear down the hall. Jenine was gazing up at Calder Red Cloud with a sense of awe.

Joseph came upon the petroglyphs unexpectedly. The ancient carvings adorned the face of a rock varnished by years of wind and rain and sun. He bent close, tracing the artwork with his fingertips. Some of the lines were merely squiggles to him, but some of them were obviously hunting scenes depicting warriors with weapons lifted high, following the trail of animals that roamed freely over the land.

Joseph surveyed his surroundings. The buttes were stark, barren, forbidding. Such an environment would test the skills and fortitude of even the most ingenious people. It was incredible to Joseph that his ancestors had not only survived in such a place but had developed a culture.

Something stirred in him—a sense of pride, an emerging affinity for a mighty people called the Sioux.

He studied the petroglyphs until deep shadows fell on the rugged walls, then he built a fire and heated his can of pork and beans. When the last ember died, he lay on his bedroll and listened to the plaintive call of a canyon wren and the haunting whisper of raven wings as those dark birds sought shelter from the night.

Or was it the song of ancient spirits?

By the time Callie left the clinic, Calder had gathered the entire family at Callie's house. He was sitting in a rocking chair in her living room, holding forth, while Jenine sat at his elbow in rapt attention.

Relief flooded Callie, and she paused in the doorway to pull herself together before she joined her family. She saw them as a beloved unit but also as dear individuals— Ellen with her refined ways and her lyrical Southern drawl that years of living in the White Mountains couldn't erase, Eric with his genteel ways and easy smile, Brenda with her maternal glow and soft exclamations of joy, the twins with their devilish grins and their capacity for wonder, and Calder...

Who could reduce him to mere words? He was a tree, a rock, a mountain. The source of their strength, the root of their courage, the wellspring of their love.

How would Jenine see them?

Her father looked up, caught Callie's eye and winked.

"Come in, Callie, and join us. I was just telling Jenine how Apache scouts helped the U.S. Army capture Geronimo—then how they got sent to a military prison down in Florida for their troubles."

Calder loved history, especially the history of his people, and took every opportunity to expound. The family, of course, loved listening to his stories, and apparently so did Jenine.

She turned a radiant smile in Callie's direction.

"Your father has royally entertained me today. I feel as if I've walked through the pages of history."

The door of opportunity yawned open, and Callie walked through.

"As children, Eric and I spent hours at our father's knee enthralled by the world he opened up to us, not only the world of history but the world of nature and of science."

Callie stood at her father's chair and draped her arm over his shoulders.

"Calder Red Cloud is one of the smartest people I've ever known. I'm lucky to be his daughter, and Eric's offspring are lucky to be his grandchildren."

Jenine's laughter was low and throaty—and genuine.

"You don't have to convince me. After what I've seen here today, I can wholeheartedly recommend that Ricky be placed with you."

Callie was too overcome to speak. Calder squeezed her hand, while Ellen and Brenda started crying.

Eric spoke for the family. "Thank you, Miss Rayborn. I promise the Red Clouds will not betray your trust."

"Don't thank me yet. I can only recommend. There is still an entire board who has to give the stamp of approval. And then, of course, there is all the legal red tape."

"It's done," Calder said. "Our hearts are singing." He stood up and offered his arms to Ellen and Jenine. "Now we will eat."

Everything was going to be perfect, Callie thought. Almost. There was one essential element missing.

"Joseph," she whispered.

Chapter Twenty-Five

It was time.

In the night Joseph had felt the tug of ancient spirits. When the fingers of dawn lay across the land, he put the sacred pipe and his father's sacred bundle into a knapsack, then followed the winding path of the stream to its source: the mouth of a crystal cave.

Bending down so he would fit through the opening, Joseph stepped into another world. Huge gypsum formations hung from the ceiling in a curtain of crystal. Sparkling spires rose up from the floor, creating a wonderland effect.

The crystals gave off an eerie glow, and even in the complete absence of light, Joseph had no trouble finding his way. Climbing over crystals, he followed the stream through a maze of tunnels that opened into an enormous chamber.

Mists rose from the lake in the center of the chamber,

and beyond the sparkling waters stood a stage carved by nature.

This is the place, Joseph thought.

He stripped, then plunged into the lake. The water was warm and soothing. It was easy to see why his ancestors had believed the springs of the Black Hills contained healing powers.

Joseph gave himself up to the waters, drifting, floating, dreaming until at last his mind was emptied of everything. The light in the cave became a living, breathing entity, sparking from one crystal to the next, moving in patterns that mesmerized.

Joseph climbed out of the lake and took the sacred pipe from his knapsack. The red clay bowl was warm to his touch, even before he lit it, and the mists rising from the lake took on the form of the White Buffalo Woman.

Slowly Joseph drew on the pipe. White Buffalo Woman vanished in the mists, and the crystals undulated in a dance of light and shadow.

"I seek the truth," Joseph said, then he closed his eyes and listened to the music of his soul.

In the midst of the soul symphony, Callie appeared, standing on a distant shore, reaching out to him. Joseph called to her, but she didn't hear. Wind whipped waves on the surface of the lake, and out of the waves came children with golden skin and Callie's blue eyes.

Tears blurred Joseph's vision, and his heart cried for a love lost. The embers burned low in the red clay bowl of the pipe, and Joseph took one final draw.

Suddenly the swirling lake mists became a hawk. The giant bird flew straight to Callie, then stood over her with wings outspread—protector, lover, friend.

Joseph bowed his head and wept.

When he emerged from the cave, bright sunlight momentarily blinded him. He closed his eyes, giving his vision time to adjust. And when he opened them he saw the hawk, hovering over his campsite.

Mesmerized, Joseph watched as the great bird lifted toward the sky. A thermal pocket caught the hawk, and as he soared upward, a single feather tore lose. It drifted downward, slowly downward, until it lay at Joseph's feet.

Calder and Ellen insisted on going with Callie when she flew down to Texas for her final interview with the board, and nothing she could say would dissuade them.

"I want to meet my grandson," Calder said.

"That's premature, Dad. The board hasn't approved my application."

"He's going to be a Red Cloud, and I'm going to see him."

Callie looked to her mother for support, but Ellen merely smiled and patted Calder's cheek.

"Your father has spoken, Callie."

Sometimes having an icon for a father could be a pain, but Callie didn't tell anybody except her brother. Eric laughed heartily.

"You've got a case of the jitters, Callie. That's all. Besides, Calder Red Cloud is seldom wrong."

Eric's words turned out to be prophetic. Two days later, standing in a Texas courtroom flanked by Ellen and Calder, Callie heard the judge say, "Congratulations, Dr. Callie Red Cloud. You have yourself a son."

Ever predictable, her mother cried. And to her surprise, so did Callie.

Calder hugged them both, wiped their tears, then beamed at everybody in the courtroom.

"I'm going to take my grandson home."

* * *

Ricky hadn't been told about the legal proceedings. Callie hadn't wanted to build his hopes up, then have them dashed.

She could barely contain her excitement. Not only was she bringing him the good news that she was now his mommy, she was also bringing him two grandparents.

"Wait right here," she told her parents when they reached Ricky's room. "I want to prepare him."

Ricky was playing hide-and-seek with his teddy bear when Callie went in.

"Come find me, Homer," he called.

Ricky stood in full view with his face to the wall and his hands over his eyes. He was thinner than when she'd last seen him, his arms skinny little sticks and his shoulder blades sticking out like wings.

All of a sudden Callie was overcome. What had she done? What had made her think she could possibly care for this child? Love him, yes. Provide for him, yes. But she had absolutely no experience in raising children. She didn't know the first thing about what a four-year-old needed.

And she was attempting to do this alone.

Ricky had lost so much. He needed so much.

Callie closed her eyes and said a silent prayer for guidance and wisdom.

"I'm gonna count to ten, Homer," Ricky said. "One, two, three, four, five, seven, nine, ten. Ready or not."

He whirled around and saw Callie. For a moment he was still as a statue, then he launched himself at her, squealing.

She squatted beside him and held him close.

"Where've you been, Callie?"

"I've been in the White Mountains making a home for us." His eyes got wide. "For you and me, Ricky."

Ricky's smile lit his entire face, then suddenly he grew solemn. "I have to stay here. Miss Rayborn told me."

"Oh, honey."

She picked up the small boy and carried him to the rocking chair. One of her fondest childhood memories was of sitting on her mother's lap while Ellen sang songs and combed her hair.

Tenderly, Callie smoothed Ricky's dark hair. "You know, Miss Rayborn has been trying very hard to find a family for you. At first she thought I wouldn't be the best mother because of my job. But I gave up my job, and Miss Rayborn said that now I can be your mother."

Ricky was silent.

"Would you like that, Ricky?"

Eyes wide, he looked up at her. "For real?"

"Yes, for real. I've come to take you home with me today."

The truth finally sank in. Ricky scooted out of her lap and raced around the room, grabbing his toys.

"Can I take Homer and Pinocchio and my ball?"

"Yes. You can take everything."

"My baseball cap? Miss Rayborn said it's too big."

Callie was laughing and crying at the same time. "Yes, you can take the baseball cap. I'll help you pack everything. But first I have a surprise for you."

"Is it candy?"

"No. It's my mother and father. They will be your grandmother and grandfather."

Ricky came close and whispered. "Is he a real Indian like you?"

"Yes," Callie whispered back.

Ricky drew himself up straight and tall. "I'm not scared."

"Of course not. You're the bravest boy I know. Are you ready to meet your grandparents?"

Ricky hugged his teddy bear to his chest. "Yes," he said.

His eyes grew huge when Ellen and Calder walked into the room. And he was so solemn during the introductions that Callie was afraid she'd given him too much to handle in one day.

Ellen and Calder didn't rush him, but stood quietly letting him take everything in. Ricky looked them over, dwelling the longest on Calder.

Then he poked out his chest and announced in his loudest voice, "I got a pet spider. I'm brave."

Ellen and Calder were smitten. "Oh, honey," Ellen said, gathering him for a big hug.

Ricky tried to act nonchalant, then his thin little arms stole around Ellen's neck. But over her shoulder he was watching Calder.

"You got a horse?" he asked.

"Yes, I have many horses, one of them just the right size for you. I'll teach you to ride."

Ricky beamed. "I'm gonna name my horse Lucky."

It was late afternoon before they boarded their plane, and by the time they got home Ricky and Calder were asleep on the back seat of the Jeep Cherokee, while Ellen and Callie chatted quietly in the front.

"I'm scared, Mom."

"You'll be fine, Callie. You have good instincts." Ellen laughed. "And Brenda and I will be close by."

Callie parked the car in front of her parents' house. "Just look at them." Ricky snuggled against Calder, and Calder's chin rested on the top of Ricky's head. "They look as if they've been that way forever. It seems a shame to wake them."

"I know. But you two need to be alone." Ellen leaned over the seat and gently shook Calder's shoulder. "We're home, darling, it's time to go in."

Calder roused, then eased himself out and leaned over to kiss Callie's cheek.

"I'm proud of you, Daughter."

When she got home, Callie sat inside the car trying to decide whether to wake Ricky and let him see his new home, or whether to carry him inside and put him straight to bed.

He didn't stir when she got out of the car, so she picked him up and carried him inside. Now what? His pajamas were in the bag still in the car.

In a crisis Callie was a dynamo, making snap decisions and moving forward with the speed of light. And yet she stood in the doorway with the deadweight of a sleeping four-year-old in her arms, trying to make up her mind about his pajamas.

"Callie?" Ricky opened his eyes, then gave a big yawn. "Are we home yet?"

"Yes. We're home"

"Can I sleep in my pants?"

"Yes. We'll just take off your shoes and socks."

She tucked him in, pulled the covers up to his chin, then kissed him softly.

"Good night, Ricky. I love you."

"I didn't say my prayers. I have to say my prayers."

Callie took the tiny hand he offered, then sat on the side of his bed. Ricky squeezed his eyes shut.

"God, it's me—Ricky—and I got a new mommy. It's Callie, and she loves me." Ricky opened one eye and squinted up at Callie. "How much do you love me, Callie?"

She spread her arms as wide as they would go. "I love you this much."

Satisfied, Ricky shut his eyes once more.

"She loves me more than anybody, and I'm gonna have a horse and a granddaddy and a grandmother and lots of toys."

Suddenly uncertain, he opened his eyes to confirm this with Callie.

"Can I have lots of toys?"

"Yes. You'll have toys and books and cousins and lots of friends to play with."

Grinning, he shut his eyes again. "See, I told you, God. I told you if you'd let Callie come get me, she'd be the best mommy in the whole world."

Ricky stopped praying, and was still so long Callie thought he had fallen asleep. She'd started to leave when Ricky spoke.

"About Joe, God. Me and him's a good pair. How about lettin' him be my daddy? Amen."

Ricky's eyes popped open, and he beamed up at Callie. "Good night, Callie."

She brushed his hair back from his forehead, then planted a kiss there.

"Night, angel."

She was able to maintain her poise until she left his room. In the hallway she leaned her head against the wall and cried.

Chapter Twenty-Six

The two men sat in the gazebo talking, both with faces that looked as if they had been carved in bronze, both with a thick mane of hair, one stark white, the other jet black. They had been talking for the past hour, and in that time Calder felt as if he had come to know Joseph's soul.

Years ago he had learned to trust his instincts, and every instinct he had was telling him that at last, here was a man worthy of his daughter.

"This is not an easy task you have set for yourself," Calder said.

"That's the understatement of the year. Your daughter is not only brilliant and beautiful, she is also stubborn. But I am going to win her if it takes the rest of my life."

"That's exactly what I told myself about her mother. Let me tell you something about Callie. It's the same thing Ellen's father told me many years ago—her bark is worse than her bite."

Joseph was quick to laugh, and his laughter was hearty. Calder liked that in a man. Callie needed somebody to laugh with.

"Then we are in agreement," Joseph said. "No one else will know I am here, especially Ricky."

"I've been promising to take him on a camping trip. This is the perfect time to go." Thinking about the little boy, Calder broke into spontaneous laughter. "We'll ride double on Sugarplum. He's going to argue with me, of course. After three lessons he thinks he's big enough to ride Lucky anywhere he wants to go. When he loses that argument, he's going to insist we ride that spawn of the devil, Thunderbolt."

Joseph narrowed his eyes. "I was right. You deliberately chose that stallion for me."

Calder's eyes twinkled. "How else was I going to know if you're a man?"

They both stood facing each other, two tall men in complete accord.

"Thank you," Joseph said.

Calder put his hand on the younger man's shoulder.

"You have my blessing. May the Great Spirit guide you, Joseph Swift Hawk."

When Calder first suggested the camping trip, Callie hadn't been enthusiastic. Ricky was just getting settled in, she'd argued. Wasn't it too soon? What if he had an accident? What if he missed Callie?

In typical Calder fashion, her father overrode all her protests, and the two of them had set out early that morning. With Ellen spending every day at Brenda's through the last few weeks of her pregnancy and Eric down at the newspaper office, Callie felt as if she had the entire Red Cloud compound to herself.

There was the clinic, of course, but that was business, not family. Besides, the population of the village was on a wellness streak, and Callie spent only a couple of hours a day at the clinic. Doug Brenner insisted she didn't have to come at all.

"Take some time off, Callie," he said. "Get to know your son."

Today she'd taken the younger doctor at his word. And she was glad. It felt good to be down on her knees digging in the dirt. Nearby, her garden cart was filled with annuals. Callie had a vision of her garden as a rainbow of color.

Sweat dripped under the brim of her garden hat and ran in a streak down the side of her cheek. Callie brushed at it with the back of her hand, then sat back on her heels to survey her handiwork. The annuals she had planted looked as if they had grown there naturally, which was exactly what she wanted.

Nothing stiff and formal for Callie. She liked all things wild.

Out of nowhere a feather drifted downward and landed at her feet. She glanced up into the sky, but there was no bird in sight.

"Strange," she muttered.

She'd picked up her trowel and started to dig when something caught her eye. A dark band with a white tip.

The red-tailed hawk.

"Hello, Callie."

His voice pierced her heart like knives. Joseph. After all these weeks.

She was grateful for the trowel. It gave her something to hold on to as she stood to face him.

His hair was longer than when she'd last seen him. He was leaner. More at ease. As if he had somehow become more comfortable in his own skin.

The physical impact of Joseph screamed along her nerves, and her heart hammered so hard she wondered if he could hear. A million questions raced through her mind. Why was he here? What did he want? What did he know?

And what about the feather?

She gripped the trowel so hard her knuckles turned white. "Hello, Joseph."

His eyes swept over her, and the hunger in them nearly drove Callie mad. She strengthened her resolve.

She was not going to let her heart rule her head. Not this time. Now she had Ricky to think of.

Smiling, Joseph reached out to touch her cheek. "You have a smudge...right there."

His fingers made contact, and her skin caught fire. She was going to jerk away, in a minute, when she could breathe again.

As if he'd read her thoughts, he bracketed her face and held her still.

"You told me never to touch you again unless I mean it." His eyes were deep and dark and full of secrets as his thumbs circled her chin. "I mean it, Callie."

Could she believe him? Did she dare? For one glorious summer he had been her Hawk, and then he'd left. How many times would a broken heart mend?

"I've come to claim you as my own."

"To claim me?"

She had a vision of a savage warrior tossing her over his stallion and riding off with her. The idea was positively the most antiquated thing she'd heard in years. Perfectly barbaric. And absolutely thrilling.

She kept that part to herself.

"You and Ricky," Joseph added.

Ricky. Of course, that had to be it. He wanted the child.

And if he knew about Ricky, then he knew about her leaving the Center for Disease Control.

She stepped back, a woman whose heart had suddenly frozen over.

"To get the child you have to take the woman. Is that it, Joseph? I'm just part of the bargain."

"Callie, Callie." He reached for her, but she slapped his hand away. "I know how this must look to you."

"Do you? Do you have any idea how it looks, Joseph? I leave virology and presto, a major obstacle is removed. Then, low and behold, I get Ricky, and suddenly you see a way to have a wonderful little boy and a bed partner, too."

Something moved in his eyes, something dangerous.

"Bravo, Dr. Joseph Swift." She applauded, then stalked toward her house. Majestically, she hoped. At least her head was high, her back straight and her eyes dry. What more could she ask?

She had gained the rose arbor when his voice stopped her cold.

"Hawk," he said. "My name is Hawk."

For a moment he thought she was going to come back to him, but Callie kept on walking. Joseph wasn't defeated, not by a long shot.

Callie had more spunk in one little finger than most women had in their entire bodies. Winning her was not going to be easy.

He watched until she was at her house, grinned when she slammed the door, then knelt beside her gardening cart. It was full of flowers whose names he didn't know.

He picked up a small pot, ripped out the plant and plunged it into the hole she'd dug. Then he grabbed another. He could do this. He was bound to have some of his mother's gardening talent.

Besides, he was a full-blood. A by-God-vision-inspired Sioux. His ancestors had lived off the land. He could certainly plant a few puny flowers.

He glanced toward the house, and saw the curtain fall back into place.

Good, Callie was watching. He wanted her to know that he didn't plan to go away. Not now. Not ever.

Joseph Swift Hawk had come to stay.

The man had gone mad.

Callie had wanted her flowers to look as if Mother Nature planted them, and by George, she'd gotten her wish. They looked as if they'd been dumped into her garden by a tornado. Or at the very least, a strong wind.

Callie let the curtain fall back, then fixed herself a good strong cup of tea. Let him stew out there in the hot sun. Let him starve. She was not about to be part of anybody's bargain package.

She took a bracing sip of tea. The curtain fluttered in the breeze.

What was Joseph doing now? Resisting the urge to look, she sipped her tea.

Hawk. He'd said his name was Hawk.

Callie's heart took wings. Lord, how she loved the man, no matter what his name.

Curiosity got the best of her, and she peeked out the window. Joseph was sitting on her garden bench with his back to the house. Funny behavior for a man who'd come to win a woman.

Restless, her nerves as taut as piano wire, Callie carried her tea through the house in search of a good book. Anything to take her mind off the warrior in her garden.

She was reaching for a book when the phone rang.

"Callie..." It was Peg, out of breath. "I couldn't wait any longer to tell you the news."

"You know the baby's gender?"

"No, not yet. It's about Joseph. He's back in America."

In my backyard, Callie thought, but she didn't say so.

"In Atlanta, at the Center for Disease Control," Peg added.

"Visiting? Consulting?"

"Bingo! He's a consultant now, both at the institute in Italy and at the center here in Atlanta."

Callie had to sit down. "Then he's not leaving the field?"

"Lord, no. What would we do without him?"

"He'll still be living in Italy, I suppose." Callie tried to keep her voice casual. "Or Atlanta."

"No, he said something about living out West." Callie's heart stood still. "Callie...are you there?"

"I'm here, Peg. I'm fine."

"You don't sound fine. What's going on?"

"Joseph is in my garden."

There was a long silence at the other end of the line, then Peg's voice, tender and wise.

"Is that the only place he is, Callie?"

"No...he's in my heart."

Peg sighed. "Lord, I love *love.*"

Callie couldn't read, of course, not after the phone call. Besides, she was hungry.

She went into the kitchen, sliced apples and cheese, then made herself a hearty sandwich. The wonderful thing about gardening was that gardeners burned lots of calories.

Callie pressed her hands against her concave belly, and was filled with an unaccountable sadness. Brenda was huge in her pregnancy, and afterward she would still have the nicely rounded belly of a woman who has borne children.

"Empty womb syndrome," Callie said. That's what was wrong with her. Joseph was in her garden, planting, enriching Mother Earth.

He was good at that.

Her hands folded over her flat belly, Callie stood at the kitchen sink, watching him and remembering how they had stood together in Texas, cocooned by the blanket, Ricky between them. A family.

It had felt so natural, so right, as if they would stay that way forever, a unit forged by love, a unit that would expand over the years to make room for the children that would surely come.

Emptiness coiled in Callie's belly, and she knew her need wasn't for food. The truth struck her with such clarity that she wondered why she had wasted all these weeks.

Everything she wanted in life was standing in her garden. Her home, her family, her future were wrapped up in a tall man whose black eyes flashed in the sun.

So what was she doing in the kitchen?

Joseph finished writing the poem, then laid it on the garden bench. Now what? He didn't know how to court a woman. Good lord, he was forty years old. It had been years since he'd wooed and won Maria.

And Callie was a different kind of woman altogether. Untamed, high-spirited, exciting.

To see her was to want her. Every time they met, they got swept up in the wild river of passion, and everything else fell by the wayside.

"It's going to be different this time," he vowed to himself.

And yet, their bodies spoke a language that needed no words.

He glanced toward the house. Somewhere inside was the woman he loved above all things, his heart, his life, his soul.

And here he was, sitting in the garden alone. Galvanized, Joseph bolted from the curving stone bench, and started toward the house.

The screen door popped open as Callie flew out the door, arms wide-open.

Suddenly he was running. They met at the rose arbor, met and merged.

"I've been such a fool," she said. "I don't know why I..."

He stopped her confession with a kiss. Lips blended, bodies swayed, hearts merged. Love welled up in Joseph, and he conveyed all that was in his heart in a kiss so tender it brought tears. They wet his cheeks, and he couldn't tell if they were his or hers.

"I've waited so long for you," she whispered. "A lifetime."

"I came for you, Callie, only you. If you were in the midst of an outbreak on the Ivory Coast, I would still come to claim you."

He kissed her throat, her cheek, her eyes. Sighing, she leaned toward him.

"Ricky is a bonus," he added, "an unexpected surprise."

"You didn't know about him?"

"No. I had planned for the two of us to get him. Later."

"I love you Callie." He captured her lips once more, and they were caught up in a magic so powerful they didn't pull apart until a curtain of darkness dropped over the land.

"I love you, Joseph Swift."

"Hawk."

"I love you by any name."

Surrounded by the fragrance of her grandmother's roses, Joseph drew Callie down to the soft rich earth underneath the arbor, and there they pledged their love to one another in a ritual as old as time.

Afterward, he brushed the bits of grass from her hair and kissed her lips and smiled into those blue eyes that he had never been able to put out of his mind, not for one single moment since the day they'd met.

"We always seem to end up coupled in the arms of Mother Earth," he said. "Do you think we'll ever make love in a real bed?"

"I'd bet on it."

Smiling softly, she took his hand and led him inside.

Chapter Twenty-Seven

When Callie woke up she saw four things on the pillow next to hers—a note, Joseph's harmonica, the feather of a hawk and a single red rose. Dew still clung to the petals.

Smiling she unfolded the note. It was a poem written in Joseph's bold hand:

The rose blooms because you smile upon it,
    and the sun pales beside the glow of your skin.
Your laughter is life's blood, and your love
    the air I breathe.
With you I am Hawk,
    soaring toward Father Sky,
    covering you with mighty wings,
    planting my seed deep in the womb
    that will nourish my children.
With you, I live.

Callie felt the hot sting of tears. Her love for Joseph swelled so that she pressed her hand over her heart to hold it all in.

There was movement deep in a corner of the bedroom the morning sun had not yet risen, and Joseph stepped out of the shadows, wonderfully, magnificently naked.

"I wanted to watch you unobserved." Joseph sat beside her on the bed and cupped her face. "Do you like my gifts?"

"Oh, Joseph. I love them." She pressed the hawk feather to her lips. "Every one of them."

"When my ancestors set out to win a woman's hand, they brought ponies."

His choice of words was not lost on her. Callie's heart stood still.

"I don't think I could fit a pony in the bedroom," she said.

"Or a nice buffalo hide." He was smiling.

"I prefer cool clean sheets."

"How about warm rumpled ones?" He pressed her back against the sheets.

"As long as you're in them." She wound her arms around his neck and drew him close.

He tasted her lips, found them sweet beyond imagining, and for a moment all talk was suspended.

"My gifts have a practical purpose," he said, finally. "Besides being a slightly battered, world-weary warrior's wedding gifts to his beloved."

Her body on fire, she whispered, "Tell me."

"Why don't I show you?"

Eyes gleaming, Hawk picked up the harmonica. Callie settled back against the pillows, ready for a song. Instead he circled the cool metal on her nipples. She caught a deep, ragged breath.

"Do you like that?" His hands kept up the erotic movements, and Callie nodded, moaning. "I see that you do."

Setting the harmonica aside, he took her rigid nipples deep into his mouth and suckled until she was moaning and wet with need.

Then he reached for the rose.

One by one he tore the rose petals apart. The first he placed on her lips, the second over her heart, the third on her navel, and the fourth in that deep secret place he had branded his own.

And one by one he claimed them. His mouth closed over hers, and for a small eternity he nibbled at the rose petal and all it covered. Then he lifted himself over her, eyes blazing as he followed the rose path downward.

Intense pleasure flooded Callie. She tangled her hands into his hair and arched upward like a fish.

"Callie, Callie, my love," he murmured. His eyes glowing, he finally lifted his head.

"Fly with me," he whispered.

"Yes," she said.

And she did.

She opened herself like blossoms in her grandmother's garden, opened her heart, her body, her mind for the magnificent Sioux who thrust himself deep into her womb and planted his seed.

Languid, sated, she lay against the pillows while he smiled into her eyes.

"What's the feather for?" she whispered.

Joseph's laughter echoed around the room.

"How I love a greedy woman."

Callie smiled. "Show me."

And he did.

Chapter Twenty-Eight

Five days after Joseph's arrival in the White Mountains, Calder and Ricky returned from their camping trip. Riding down the steep trail on Sugarplum, Ricky sang old Apache chants Calder had taught him.

Callie and Joseph heard them coming.

Calder drew the docile mare to a halt in Callie's front yard, then helped his grandson off the horse. Ricky took the front porch steps two at a time.

"Callie, listen to this." He burst through the front door. "Granddaddy taught me…"

His sneakers skidded on the floor, and for a moment he was dumbstruck. Then he launched himself at Joseph, who caught him and spun him high in the air.

"How are you doing, pal?"

Ricky, still speechless, could do nothing but laugh.

Calder came into the room and put his arm around Callie's waist.

"Looks like things went well with the two of you, Daughter."

"You knew?"

"I not only knew, I gave my blessing. Don't look so thunderstruck. Did you think a man like Hawk would not ask me for my daughter's hand in marriage?"

He kissed Callie's flushed cheek. "I said yes. Did you?"

"He hasn't asked yet. At least, not in so many words."

In the middle of the room, Joseph and Ricky still spun round and round, both dizzy with excitement and laughter.

"Action. That's what counts."

The human whirligig finally came to a halt. Breathless, Ricky looked up at Joseph with pure adoration and a smile as big as Texas.

"I knew you'd come," he told Joseph.

"You did?"

"Yeah. Me 'n God talked about it." Ricky cocked his head to one side. "Are you gonna be my daddy?"

Joseph had never known it was possible for a man's heart to be so full. Unbidden, he had a spirit vision, and in it he saw the Hawk spreading his protective wings over the woman he loved, and her children.

His eyes sought Callie, the center of his universe, his heart, his life, his future.

"If you and Callie will have me," he said.

"Yes, yes, yes," Ricky chanted, dancing about the room.

Callie smiled. "Yes," she said. "Now and forever."

Joseph strode across the room and brushed the object he'd pulled out of his pocket across her lips.

It was the feather of a hawk.

*   *   *   *   *

If you enjoyed what you just read,
then we've got an offer you can't resist!

Take 2 bestselling love stories FREE!

Plus get a FREE surprise gift!

Clip this page and mail it to Silhouette Reader Service™

IN U.S.A.	IN CANADA
3010 Walden Ave.	P.O. Box 609
P.O. Box 1867	Fort Erie, Ontario
Buffalo, N.Y. 14240-1867	L2A 5X3

YES! Please send me 2 free Silhouette Special Edition® novels and my free surprise gift. Then send me 6 brand-new novels every month, which I will receive months before they're available in stores. In the U.S.A., bill me at the bargain price of $3.57 plus 25¢ delivery per book and applicable sales tax, if any*. In Canada, bill me at the bargain price of $3.96 plus 25¢ delivery per book and applicable taxes**. That's the complete price and a savings of over 10% off the cover prices—what a great deal! I understand that accepting the 2 free books and gift places me under no obligation ever to buy any books. I can always return a shipment and cancel at any time. Even if I never buy another book from Silhouette, the 2 free books and gift are mine to keep forever. So why not take us up on our invitation. You'll be glad you did!

235 SEN CNFD
335 SEN CNFE

Name	(PLEASE PRINT)	
Address	Apt.#	
City	State/Prov.	Zip/Postal Code

* Terms and prices subject to change without notice. Sales tax applicable in N.Y.
** Canadian residents will be charged applicable provincial taxes and GST.
   All orders subject to approval. Offer limited to one per household.
   ® are registered trademarks of Harlequin Enterprises Limited.

SPED99   ©1998 Harlequin Enterprises Limited

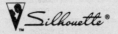

SILHOUETTE'S 20ᵀᴴ ANNIVERSARY CONTEST
OFFICIAL RULES
NO PURCHASE NECESSARY TO ENTER

1. To enter, follow directions published in the offer to which you are responding. Contest begins 1/1/00 and ends on 8/24/00 (the "Promotion Period"). Method of entry may vary. Mailed entries must be postmarked by 8/24/00, and received by 8/31/00.

2. During the Promotion Period, the Contest may be presented via the Internet. Entry via the Internet may be restricted to residents of certain geographic areas that are disclosed on the Web site. To enter via the Internet, if you are a resident of a geographic area in which Internet entry is permissible, follow the directions displayed on-line, including typing your essay of 100 words or fewer telling us "Where In The World Your Love Will Come Alive." On-line entries must be received by 11:59 p.m. Eastern Standard time on 8/24/00. Limit one e-mail entry per person, household and e-mail address per day, per presentation. If you are a resident of a geographic area in which entry via the Internet is permissible, you may, in lieu of submitting an entry on-line, enter by mail, by hand-printing your name, address, telephone number and contest number/name on an 8"x 11" plain piece of paper and telling us in 100 words or fewer "Where In The World Your Love Will Come Alive," and mailing via first-class mail to: Silhouette 20ᵗʰ Anniversary Contest, (in the U.S.) P.O. Box 9069, Buffalo, NY 14269-9069; (In Canada) P.O. Box 637, Fort Erie, Ontario, Canada L2A 5X3. Limit one 8"x 11" mailed entry per person, household and e-mail address per day. On-line and/or 8"x 11" mailed entries received from persons residing in geographic areas in which Internet entry is not permissible will be disqualified. No liability is assumed for lost, late, incomplete, inaccurate, nondelivered or misdirected mail, or misdirected e-mail, for technical, hardware or software failures of any kind, lost or unavailable network connection, or failed, incomplete, garbled or delayed computer transmission or any human error which may occur in the receipt or processing of the entries in the contest.

3. Essays will be judged by a panel of members of the Silhouette editorial and marketing staff based on the following criteria:

    Sincerity (believability, credibility)—50%

    Originality (freshness, creativity)—30%

    Aptness (appropriateness to contest ideas)—20%

    Purchase or acceptance of a product offer does not improve your chances of winning. In the event of a tie, duplicate prizes will be awarded.

4. All entries become the property of Harlequin Enterprises Ltd., and will not be returned. Winner will be determined no later than 10/31/00 and will be notified by mail. Grand Prize winner will be required to sign and return Affidavit of Eligibility within 15 days of receipt of notification. Noncompliance within the time period may result in disqualification and an alternative winner may be selected. All municipal, provincial, federal, state and local laws and regulations apply. Contest open only to residents of the U.S. and Canada who are 18 years of age or older, and is void wherever prohibited by law. Internet entry is restricted solely to residents of those geographical areas in which Internet entry is permissible. Employees of Torstar Corp., their affiliates, agents and members of their immediate families are not eligible. Taxes on the prizes are the sole responsibility of winners. Entry and acceptance of any prize offered constitutes permission to use winner's name, photograph or other likeness for the purposes of advertising, trade and promotion on behalf of Torstar Corp. without further compensation to the winner, unless prohibited by law. Torstar Corp and D.L. Blair, Inc., their parents, affiliates and subsidiaries, are not responsible for errors in printing or electronic presentation of contest or entries. In the event of printing or other errors which may result in unintended prize values or duplication of prizes, all affected contest materials or entries shall be null and void. If for any reason the Internet portion of the contest is not capable of running as planned, including infection by computer virus, bugs, tampering, unauthorized intervention, fraud, technical failures, or any other causes beyond the control of Torstar Corp. which corrupt or affect the administration, secrecy, fairness, integrity or proper conduct of the contest, Torstar Corp. reserves the right, at its sole discretion, to disqualify any individual who tampers with the entry process and to cancel, terminate, modify or suspend the contest or the Internet portion thereof. In the event of a dispute regarding an on-line entry, the entry will be deemed submitted by the authorized holder of the e-mail account submitted at the time of entry. Authorized account holder is defined as the natural person who is assigned to an e-mail address by an Internet access provider, on-line service provider or other organization that is responsible for arranging e-mail address for the domain associated with the submitted e-mail address.

5. Prizes: Grand Prize—a $10,000 vacation to anywhere in the world. Travelers (at least one must be 18 years of age or older) or parent or guardian if one traveler is a minor, must sign and return a Release of Liability prior to departure. Travel must be completed by December 31, 2001, and is subject to space and accommodations availability. Two hundred (200) Second Prizes—a two-book limited edition autographed collector set from one of the Silhouette Anniversary authors: Nora Roberts, Diana Palmer, Linda Howard or Annette Broadrick (value $10.00 each set). All prizes are valued in U.S. dollars.

6. For a list of winners (available after 10/31/00), send a self-addressed, stamped envelope to: Harlequin Silhouette 20ᵗʰ Anniversary Winners, P.O. Box 4200, Blair, NE 68009-4200.

Contest sponsored by Torstar Corp., P.O. Box 9042, Buffalo, NY 14269-9042.

ENTER FOR
A CHANCE TO WIN*
Silhouette's 20th Anniversary Contest

Tell Us Where in the World
You Would Like *Your* Love To Come Alive...
And We'll Send the Lucky Winner There!

Silhouette wants to take you wherever
your happy ending can come true.

Here's how to enter: Tell us, in 100 words or less,
where you want to go to make your love come alive!

In addition to the grand prize, there will be 200
runner-up prizes, collector's-edition book sets
autographed by one of the Silhouette anniversary
authors: **Nora Roberts, Diana Palmer,
Linda Howard** or **Annette Broadrick**.

DON'T MISS YOUR CHANCE TO WIN!
ENTER NOW! No Purchase Necessary

Silhouette®
Where love comes alive™

Name: _____

Address: _____

City: _____ State/Province: _____

Zip/Postal Code: _____

Mail to Harlequin Books: **In the U.S.**: P.O. Box 9069, Buffalo, NY
14269-9069; **In Canada**: P.O. Box 637, Fort Erie, Ontario, L4A 5X3

PS20CON_R

#1303 MAN…MERCENARY…MONARCH—Joan Elliott Pickart
Royally Wed

In the blink of an eye, John Colton discovered he was a Crown Prince, a brand-new father…and a man on the verge of falling for a woman in *his* royal family's employ. Yet trust—and love—didn't come easily to this one-time mercenary who desperately wanted to be son, brother, father…*husband?*

#1304 DR. MOM AND THE MILLIONAIRE—Christine Flynn
Prescription: Marriage

No woman had been able to get the powerful Chase Harrington anywhere near an altar. Then again, this confirmed bachelor had never met someone like the charmingly fascinating Dr. Alexandra Larson, a woman whose tender loving care promised to heal him, body, heart…and soul.

#1305 WHO'S THAT BABY?—Diana Whitney
So Many Babies

Johnny Winterhawk did what any red-blooded male would when he found a baby on his doorstep—he panicked. Pediatrician Claire Davis rescued him by offering her hand in a marriage of convenience…and then showed him just how real a family they could be.

#1306 CATTLEMAN'S COURTSHIP—Lois Faye Dyer

Experience made Quinn Bowdrie a tough man of the land who didn't need anybody. That is, until he met the sweetly tempting Victoria Denning, the only woman who could teach this stubborn rancher the pleasures of courtship.

#1307 THE MARRIAGE BASKET—Sharon De Vita
The Blackwell Brothers

Rina Roberts had her heart set on adopting her orphaned nephew. But the boy's godfather, Hunter Blackwell, stood in her way. Their love for the child drew them together and Rina knew that not only did the handsome doctor hold the key to Billy's future—but also to her own heart.

#1308 FALLING FOR AN OLDER MAN—Trisha Alexander
Callahans & Kin

Sheila Callahan dreamed of picket fences and wedding rings, but Jack Kinsella, the man of her dreams, wasn't the slightest bit interested in commitment, especially not to his best friend's younger sister. But one night together created more than just passion….